PU

Ctrl-Z

Andrew Norriss was born in Scotland in 1947, went to un   ty in Ireland and taught history in a sixth-form   e in England for ten years before becoming a ful   writer. In the course of twenty years, he has   and co-written some hundred and fifty epis   situation comedies and children's drama for   on. He has also written many books for chil   including *Aquila*, which won the Whitbread Chi   s Book of the Year in 1997, and *The Unluckiest Boy   e World*, which won the Lancashire Schools Fan   Book Prize in 2007.

H   s very contentedly with his wife and two chil   a village in Hampshire, where he acts in the   matic society (average age sixty-two), sings in t   h choir (average age seventy-two) and for real e   ment travels to the cinema in Basingstoke.

orriss has a wonderful light comic touch'
Sunday Telegraph

' ndrew Norriss keeps the reader hooked through
narrative that is both comic and touching'
writeaway.org.uk on *The Unluckiest Boy in the World*

Books by Andrew Norriss

AQUILA
BERNARD'S WATCH
MATT'S MILLION
THE PORTAL
THE TOUCHSTONE
THE UNLUCKIEST BOY IN THE WORLD
CTRL-Z

ANDREW NORRISS

Ctrl-Z

PUFFIN

PUFFIN BOOKS

Published by the Penguin Group
Penguin Books Ltd, 80 Strand, London WC2R ORL, England
Penguin Group (USA) Inc., 375 Hudson Street, New York, New York 10014, USA
Penguin Group (Canada), 90 Eglinton Avenue East, Suite 700, Toronto, Ontario, Canada M4P 2Y3
(a division of Pearson Penguin Canada Inc.)
Penguin Ireland, 25 St Stephen's Green, Dublin 2, Ireland (a division of Penguin Books Ltd)
Penguin Group (Australia), 250 Camberwell Road, Camberwell, Victoria 3124, Australia
(a division of Pearson Australia Group Pty Ltd)
Penguin Books India Pvt Ltd, 11 Community Centre, Panchsheel Park, New Delhi – 110 017, India
Penguin Group (NZ), 67 Apollo Drive, Rosedale, North Shore 0632, New Zealand
(a division of Pearson New Zealand Ltd)
Penguin Books (South Africa) (Pty) Ltd, 24 Sturdee Avenue, Rosebank,
Johannesburg 2196, South Africa

Penguin Books Ltd, Registered Offices: 80 Strand, London WC2R ORL, England

puffinbooks.com

First published 2009
1

Set in Monotype Plantin by Palimpsest Book Production Limited,
Grangemouth, Stirlingshire
Made and printed in England by Clays Ltd, St Ives plc

British Library Cataloguing in Publication Data
A CIP catalogue record for this book is available from the British Library

ISBN: 978-0-141-32429-6

www.greenpenguin.co.uk

Penguin Books is committed to a sustainable future
for our business, our readers and our planet.
The book in your hands is made from paper
certified by the Forest Stewardship Council.

For my wonderful god-daughter, Beth,
who seems to make no mistakes at all.
And thank you, Johnny, for the idea.

CHAPTER ONE

It was a Saturday morning and Alex was sitting at the desk in his bedroom, when his father called up to say there was a parcel for him. A parcel sounded interesting, Alex thought, and he hurried downstairs to the kitchen, where his father was studying the label on a box about the size of a small suitcase.

'It's from Godfather John,' he said, as Alex appeared. 'I suppose it's a birthday present.'

Alex's birthday was not for another three months, but presents from Godfather John could arrive at any time in the year, and when they did they were usually . . . unusual.

Last year's present, for instance, had been a Make Your Own Explosions Kit, which Alex still wasn't allowed to play with, and the year before that his godfather had sent a pair of ferrets, with detailed instructions on how to use them to catch rabbits.

'Perhaps we should open it outside,' said Mr Howard doubtfully, remembering the ferrets, but Alex was already tearing off the brown paper and pulling open the lid of the box.

Inside was a battered black case containing a laptop computer.

'Goodness,' said his father. 'How very generous.' He peered into the empty box. 'Is there a card with it? Or a letter?'

Alex was rather disappointed. A laptop computer might sound like an exciting present to get, but this was not, he could see, a new machine. It was old, with spots on it that looked like bits of somebody's lunch. It probably wouldn't be able to do half the things that Alex could do on the computer his parents had given him for Christmas. As presents went, an old laptop was a lot less exciting than a Make Your Own Explosions Kit or a pair of ferrets.

'Are you going to try it out?' asked his father.

'He's not trying out anything till he's done the drying-up.' Alex's mother had appeared in the kitchen, wiping oil and grease off her hands on to a piece of kitchen towel. 'Could someone put the kettle on?'

Ten minutes later, when Alex had finished the drying-up, he took his computer upstairs to his room.

It might only be an old laptop, but you never knew. There might be some interesting games on it.

Sitting at his desk, he turned on the machine and a window appeared asking him to type in his name, and then to fill in the date and the time. The date was the fourteenth of May and the clock on his desk said the time was twenty-three minutes past ten, so he tapped in the numbers 10.23.

At least, that was what he meant to do.

In fact he typed in the numbers 10.03.

That wasn't really a problem, though. Alex knew that when you made a mistake on a computer, there was a very simple solution. If you pressed the Control key and then pressed Z, the computer went back to before you had made the mistake.

So that was what he did now.

He pressed Ctrl-Z.

And the computer disappeared.

It took a moment for this to sink in. After all, things *don't* just disappear – especially not computers that you've only had for ten minutes and hardly touched. Alex looked round the room and under the desk – he even looked out of the window, but there was no mistake. The laptop had vanished and there wasn't a sign of it anywhere.

He was still sitting at his desk, wondering what he should do, when his father called up from downstairs to say there was a parcel for him.

Puzzled, Alex went down to the kitchen where he found his father studying the label on a box about the size of a small suitcase.

'It's from Godfather John,' he said when he saw Alex. 'I suppose it's a birthday present.'

Alex stared at the parcel. 'It's the same as the last one!' he said.

'You mean the Make Your Own Explosions Kit?' said his father. 'No, no, that was a much bigger box.' He paused for a moment before adding doubtfully, 'Perhaps we should open it outside.'

Alex stepped forward, tore off the paper and pulled open the lid of the box. Inside was a battered black case, containing a laptop computer.

The whole thing was getting weirder by the second. 'It's another computer,' said Alex. 'Why would he send me another computer?'

'Well, he probably didn't know that we gave you one for Christmas,' said his father, picking a bit of dried egg off the lid. 'And this one's a laptop. Which means you can have it upstairs in your room, if you like. Are you going to try it out?'

'He's not trying out anything till he's done the drying-up.' Alex's mother had appeared in the kitchen, wiping oil and grease off her hands on to a piece of kitchen towel. 'Could someone put the kettle on?'

'I've already done the drying-up,' said Alex. 'I

did it just –' he stopped. There on the draining board were all the breakfast dishes. Not more dishes that had been put there since he did the drying-up, but *exactly the same* dishes as before. As if someone had carefully taken them back out of the cupboard, got them wet under a tap and put them out for him to do all over again.

He was beginning to think that the whole world had gone mad – and then he saw the clock.

The clock on the kitchen wall said that the time was eight minutes past ten.

A faint suspicion of what must have happened stirred in his mind. It was quite impossible, of course, and yet . . . and yet . . .

Twelve minutes later, when Alex had finished doing the drying-up for the second time, he was back at his desk in his bedroom with the laptop open in front of him.

After he had turned it on, a window appeared asking him to type in his name, and then to fill in the date and the time. He typed in his name, filled in the date, 14 May, and then the time.

The clock on his desk said the time was twenty-two minutes past ten, but that was not the number he tapped in. Instead, he did exactly what he had done before and carefully tapped in the wrong time – 10.03 – and then pressed the Control key and Z.

The computer disappeared, and Alex sat there, waiting.

He didn't have to wait long.

It was only a minute or so before his father's voice came floating up from downstairs to say there was a parcel for him.

The clock on the kitchen wall said that the time was four minutes past ten. Alex's father was studying the label on a box about the size of a small suitcase and saying, 'It's from Godfather John. I suppose it's a birthday present.'

And then everything happened again. It was the strangest feeling, watching the events unfold – opening the box, finding the computer, his father's surprise, his mother coming in from the garage and saying he had to do the drying-up for the *third* time.

Finally, he was back at his desk in his bedroom, typing his name and address into the computer and then filling in the date and the time . . .

Well, not the time. Not just yet.

Because the time was the secret, he was sure of that. When he typed in 10.03 he had gone back to 10.03, but did that mean if he typed in a different time he would go back to that one instead?

There was only one way to find out.

The clock on the right-hand side of his desk said the time was 10.21. He tapped in 10.20 on the keyboard, then moved the clock from the right-hand side of his desk to the left before pushing down the Control key and tapping the Z.

Instantly, the clock disappeared from the left-hand side of the desk and was back on the right.

And it said the time was 10.20.

He did the same thing again, just to check. This time, as an experiment, as well as moving the clock from one side of the desk to the other, he moved some books from the shelves by the window to the middle of the floor, and a pair of slippers on to the bed. Sitting back at his desk, the clock said the time was 10.22. He tapped 10.20 into the computer and pressed Ctrl-Z again.

In an instant, the clock had moved back to its original position, the slippers were back under the bed and the books were back on the shelf. Everything was back to exactly how it had been at 10.20.

It was extraordinary. It was the most extraordinary thing that had ever happened to him, Alex thought. It was hard to believe, but it seemed that if you put a time into the computer and pressed Ctrl-Z, you went back to that time.

It was so hard to believe, he thought he had better try it again.

For his next experiment, he decided to make more changes than moving a few books and a pair of slippers. This time, he tipped *all* the books on to the floor, he emptied the entire contents of a box of Lego on to the carpet and then pulled his duvet and pillows off the bed for good measure. While he was pulling the duvet, he knocked his bedside light on to the floor and broke it, and for a moment he wondered how he was going to explain this to his parents. But then he realized he didn't have to explain anything. It didn't *matter* how much damage he did or what he broke because when he pressed Ctrl-Z everything would go back to how it had been before.

He was still standing there thinking about this when his father came in.

'Just wanted to see how you were getting on with –' Mr Howard paused, taking in the bedding on the floor, the Lego scattered on the carpet and the broken bedside light. 'What on earth have you been doing?'

'Ah . . .' said Alex. 'Well . . .'

'You've broken the light,' said his father. 'How did that happen?'

'Um . . .'

'And why's all this stuff on the floor? What's going on?'

Alex was moving towards his desk. 'Hang on a minute,' he said. 'I just have to type in something.'

'You're not typing in anything,' said Mr Howard firmly, 'until you've explained what all this –'

But at that point Alex pressed Ctrl-Z and his father disappeared. Alex was back sitting at his desk, the duvet and pillows were back on the bed and the bedside light was back on the table, unbroken, and the clock said it was twenty minutes past ten.

Looking at the computer screen, he noticed for the first time a little envelope icon in the bottom right-hand corner. When he clicked on it, the menu screen disappeared and was replaced by an email. It said –

Dear Alex

I know you're probably thinking this is a really boring present and you've already got a much better computer, but hold your horses because this machine can do something really quite interesting!

When it asks you to fill in your details, one of the things it'll want you to do is fill in the time. You can always put in the right time, but if you put in an earlier time and press Ctrl-Z, I think the result will surprise you!

Anyway, I hope you have some fun with it and make lots of mistakes!

Your loving godfather

John Presley

PS It might be best not to mention any of this to your parents. They'd probably just take it away like they did the Explosions Kit!

Alex read the email through twice. He had no idea why Godfather John should want him to make lots of mistakes, but that was only one of several questions buzzing round his brain. Like where the laptop had come from, who had made it, and how it worked . . .

The door opened and his father came in.

'Just wanted to see how you were getting on with your birthday present,' he said. 'Does it work?'

'Yes, yes, it does,' said Alex. He stood up. 'I thought I might take it round and show Callum.'

'Won't he be busy this morning,' said Mr Howard, 'with the party?'

'That's not till this afternoon,' said Alex. He closed the lid of the laptop. 'And there's a program on here I think he'd like to see.'

He had a feeling that his friend Callum would be particularly interested in Ctrl-Z.

CHAPTER TWO

Callum lived four houses down on the other side of the road and, when Alex rang the bell, the door was opened by Mrs Bannister. Callum's mother was a large, broad-shouldered woman with an anxious expression that changed to a smile of relief when she saw Alex.

'Oh good! I was hoping you'd come round!' She put a hand on Alex's shoulder and swept him indoors. 'There's a lot to do and we need someone to keep an eye on Callum.' She led the way through the house. 'He's been all right so far, but . . . well, you know what I mean.'

Alex knew exactly what she meant. Callum was what is sometimes called 'accident-prone'. It wasn't that he did anything bad on purpose, but things seemed to happen when he was around and, if you heard that someone in the neighbourhood had fallen out of a window or electrocuted themselves with a toaster, you could be fairly certain that Callum would be involved in it somehow. However hard he tried to avoid an accident – and he tried very hard indeed – things just seemed to . . . happen.

'His father's put him in charge of the balloons,' said Mrs Bannister in a low voice as she led Alex out through the kitchen and into the back garden. She gestured nervously over to the patio where Callum was blowing up balloons with the aid of a large gas cylinder. 'I'm not sure it was wise, but at least he's where we can see him. Try to make sure he doesn't . . . *do* anything, will you?'

'OK,' said Alex, and he walked across to join his friend.

'You're early,' said Callum. 'Dad isn't picking up Lilly for an hour yet.'

Lilly was Callum's sister, and she had been in hospital for the last six weeks with a bone infection called osteomyelitis. Today she was coming home, and her parents had organized a party and invited some of her friends to help celebrate.

'I know,' said Alex. 'I came to show you this.' He reached into his bag and took out the laptop. 'I got it this morning.'

Callum frowned. 'I thought you already had a computer. Didn't you get one for Christmas?'

12

'Yes,' said Alex, 'but not like this. My godfather gave me this one, and it's . . . it's amazing.'

'Oh?' Callum picked up a balloon, attached it to the nozzle of the gas cylinder and opened the valve. 'Amazing how?'

'You won't believe me if I tell you,' said Alex, 'so I'll show you.' He sat on a garden bench and turned on the laptop.

On his way over, he had already decided that the simplest way to explain what the computer did would be for Callum to try it himself. He tapped at the keys to find the page that set the time, altered the numbers to two minutes earlier and held out the laptop to Callum.

'I've set it up for you,' he said. 'All you have to do is press Ctrl-Z.'

'Can I do it later?' Callum put a clip in the base of the balloon and tied its string to the arm of a garden chair to stop it floating away. 'Only Dad wants a hundred of these and I haven't done half that.'

'Ctrl-Z,' said Alex. 'That's all you have to do. Press Ctrl-Z.'

Callum gave a little shrug, reached forward and held down the Control key with one finger and pressed Z with another.

Alex found himself standing outside the kitchen door with Mrs Bannister.

'His father's put him in charge of the balloons,' Mrs Bannister was saying in a low voice. She gestured nervously over to the patio. 'I'm not sure it was wise, but at least he's where we can see him. Try to make sure he doesn't . . . *do* anything, will you?'

'Um . . . OK,' said Alex, and he walked across to join his friend.

'You're early,' said Callum. 'Dad isn't picking up Lilly for an hour yet.'

'You don't remember?' said Alex.

'Remember what?' Callum pointed to the bag Alex was carrying. 'What's in there?'

'It's the computer,' said Alex. 'The one I was telling you about. You really don't remember?'

'I thought you already had a computer.' Callum picked up a balloon, attached it to the nozzle of the gas cylinder and opened the valve. 'Didn't you get one for Christmas?'

'Yes, I did,' said Alex, 'but it wasn't like this one. This one . . .' He stopped, not quite sure what to say. How could you explain to someone that you had a machine that meant you could go back in time when you were the only person that ever remembered that you had?

'Dad wants me to do a hundred of these,' said Callum. He put a clip in the base of the balloon and tied it to the arm of a garden chair to stop it floating away. 'He wants them all over the garden. Pass me another, will you?'

Alex passed up another balloon from the box on the bench and Callum began filling it with gas. There had to be some way of explaining it, thought Alex, and as Callum filled balloons and chattered about an accident he had had that morning with a hedge-trimmer, he tried to think what it was.

At the bottom of the garden, Mr Bannister was trying to mow the last bit of lawn, but his mower had stopped and he couldn't get it started again.

From the open patio doors behind him came the sound of a cricket match on the television and the voice of the commentator saying Flintoff had been caught at mid-off and England still needed seventeen runs to win.

Mrs Bannister came out of the kitchen with a tray of cutlery, which she carried over to a table set out in the middle of the lawn, and called to her husband to help move it into the shade . . .

. . . And suddenly Alex knew exactly what he had to do.

He sat on the bench, opened his laptop, set the time and pressed Ctrl-Z.

'What's in there?' Callum asked, pointing to the bag Alex was carrying.

'It's a computer,' said Alex, reaching down and lifting out the laptop. 'I got it this morning.'

Callum picked up a balloon. 'I thought you already had a computer.'

'Yes, I do,' said Alex, 'but this isn't like the one I got for Christmas. This one can take you back in time. If you press Ctrl-Z on it, you go back to an earlier part of the day.'

'Ah . . .' Callum attached the balloon to the nozzle of the gas cylinder and opened the valve. 'I was going to get one of those,' he said, 'but then I thought, no, I'll save up for an invisibility cloak.'

'I know you don't believe me,' said Alex, 'but I can prove it.' He looked at his watch. 'In about five seconds your dad's lawnmower is going to stop. He'll try to get it started again, but it won't. Then the television will say Flintoff's out and England still need seventeen runs or something, and then your mother'll come out of the kitchen with a tray of stuff she'll put on the table over there and she'll ask your dad to give her a hand moving it into the shade.'

Callum stared at Alex for a moment and was about to speak when the sound of Mr Bannister's lawnmowing suddenly stopped. At the far end of the garden, they watched as he tried unsuccessfully to restart the mower.

'He's gone!' came the excited voice of the commentator from the television indoors. 'Flintoff has gone! Caught at mid-off by Pritchard and England still need seventeen runs if they are to win this match . . .'

'Could you help me move this?' Mrs Bannister called to her husband, as she put her tray on the table in the middle of the lawn. 'I think it'd be better in the shade.'

Callum turned to Alex, his mouth hanging open. 'How . . . How did you know all that?'

'Because I've done all this before,' said Alex. 'It's the computer. It lets me go back in time.' And he was about to explain how, with Ctrl-Z he could do this, when he noticed that the chair with the balloons was now three metres in the air and still rising.

The garden chair, to which Callum had carefully attached forty-three balloons filled with helium, was made of lightweight aluminium. A moment before, there had been no indication that forty-three balloons might be enough to make it float up into the air, but that was because, until then, Mojo the dog had been curled up on the seat. Seeing Mrs Bannister come out of the kitchen with a tray, however, Mojo had got down to investigate. In his experience, trays and tables meant there was a possibility of food.

Without his weight, the helium in the forty-three balloons had been enough to lift the chair into the sky and, as the boys watched, it bumped into the satellite dish on the wall just under the guttering.

There was a cry from indoors as Callum's grandfather called out to say the picture had disappeared on the television.

The balloons, with the chair swinging beneath them, continued to rise and then began drifting down the garden, carried on the breeze.

Callum's grandfather appeared on the patio. 'Something's happened to the television,' he said. 'The picture's gone. We only needed seventeen runs and –' He paused, looking round the patio. 'Where's my jacket?'

'What?' Callum tore his eyes away from the floating chair.

'I left my jacket on the back of a chair out here,' said Grandad. He looked suspiciously at Callum. 'What have you done with it?'

'I-I haven't done anything . . .' Callum sounded understandably nervous.

'Well, where is it, then?' demanded Grandad.

'It's all right!' said Alex. 'It's coming down!'

He pointed excitedly down the garden to where the chair was indeed losing height. Some of the balloons had snagged on the branches of a tree and popped, with the result that the chair, with Grandad's jacket hanging on the back, was losing height. Losing height quite rapidly.

Callum was the first to spot the danger. 'Dad!' he called out. 'Dad, watch out!'

Carrying one end of the table, Mr Bannister turned, looked around and then looked up – unfortunately just in time for the metal base of the garden chair to hit him squarely on the bridge of his nose.

With a cry, he toppled backwards into a patch of nettles as the chair continued its downward journey to land with a splash in the pond.

'My jacket!' Grandad began running down the garden. 'I've got my ticket for Australia in there!'

'Arnold!' Mrs Bannister was kneeling beside her husband who was bleeding profusely from the nose. 'Arnold, are you all right?'

Callum stared out at the scene. 'Why?' He shook his head in disbelief. 'Why do these things always happen to me?'

Alex, however, did not answer. He was sitting on the bench, tapping busily at the keys on his laptop.

'Try to make sure he doesn't . . . *do* anything, will you?' Mrs Bannister was saying.

It took Alex a moment to remember when he

was. 'Um . . . right,' he said, and walked across the patio to Callum.

'You're early,' said Callum. 'Dad isn't picking up Lilly for an hour yet.'

'I know,' said Alex. 'Now, listen. First of all, it's a mistake to tie those balloons to that chair because when the dog jumps off it's going to float away, right?'

'What? What are you talking about?' Callum looked puzzled.

'We'll do the balloons first and get round to the explanations later,' said Alex, 'and when we do, I want you to pay attention because I'm only going to explain this once more.'

Even when Alex had explained everything twice, starting with what had happened at home when the parcel containing the computer had first arrived and finishing with the chair floating off into the air, Callum did not find it easy to believe.

'You saw the balloons lift the chair?' he said.

'Yes,' said Alex patiently.

'And it knocked into the satellite dish and floated off down the garden?'

'That's right,' said Alex. 'Then the balloons punctured on some trees, the chair landed on your dad's nose and your grandad's jacket fell into the pond.'

'But I don't remember any of that.' Callum shook

his head as if it might jog a memory back into his mind. 'I don't remember anything like that at all.'

'Of course you don't,' said Alex. 'I told you. When I use Ctrl-Z, nobody except me remembers anything.'

'Yes . . .' Callum nodded doubtfully. It would be simplest to think that his friend was making the whole thing up, but apart from the fact that Alex didn't make things up, there was the problem of explaining how his friend knew about the balloons, and the lawnmower stopping, and what the score would be in the cricket on television . . .

'Can I try it?' he asked.

'You already did,' said Alex. 'It's no good. It only works for me.'

'How about,' said Callum slowly, 'if we put my name in the computer instead of yours? We can change it back to yours after,' he added hastily, seeing the look on Alex's face. 'It'd only be so I can try it.'

A little reluctantly Alex agreed, but when they tried they found it was impossible. Alex's name could not be altered. The only thing you could change on that page was the time and when Callum insisted on doing that and then pressing Ctrl-Z himself, the result was the same as before. Only Alex had any memory of going back a minute.

The trouble was that once he'd gone back in time, Callum didn't *know* that he'd tried it and was back to when he was asking if he *could* try it, and Alex had to explain that he already had, twice now, and that he would have to accept the fact that the only person affected by Ctrl-Z was Alex.

'That's a shame, that is.' Callum was visibly disappointed. 'Because there are times when something like that would be really useful to someone like me.'

'You mean like when you've had one of your accidents?'

'Yes.' Callum sat down on the bench and stared thoughtfully down the garden.

'It doesn't matter,' said Alex. 'I can do it for you. Any time something happens to you, all you have to do is tell me and I'll go back and stop it.'

Callum considered this. 'You mean, if I sat down on this bench and broke something, for instance, you could go back to before I'd done it?'

'Yes,' said Alex. 'Exactly. All you have to do is ask.' He looked at his friend. 'What have you sat on then?'

'I'm not sure.' Callum reached behind him and produced the bag Alex had brought. From inside he took out a small, squashed box, wrapped in gold paper.

'That's the welcome home present I got for Lilly,' said Alex.

'Ah . . .' Callum shook the box, which made a rattling, tinkling noise. 'Is it supposed to sound like that?'

'Not really,' said Alex. 'It was a china dog.' He reached for the computer. 'Hang on . . .'

'That's a shame, that is.' Callum was visibly disappointed. 'Because there are times when something like that would be really useful to someone like me.'

'You mean like when you've had one of your accidents?' Alex reached out to move his bag from the bench.

'Yes.' Callum sat down and stared thoughtfully down the garden. He turned to his friend. 'What are you going to do with it?'

Alex hesitated. 'I'm not sure. Godfather John said in his email I should use it to have fun and make mistakes.'

'Make mistakes?'

Alex gave a shrug. 'That's what he said.'

'I should be able to help you there,' said Callum. 'I can probably make enough mistakes for both of us.'

CHAPTER THREE

The party was a great success. When Mr Bannister came back from the hospital with Lilly, you could see how thrilled she was to be home, and how pleased she was to see the balloons and decorations spread out over the garden. Everyone cheered as she came over the grass in her wheelchair – it would be a few weeks yet before her legs had completely recovered – and for the next hour she was busy opening all her welcome home presents.

The eating and the fun and the games went on for most of the afternoon. Alex stayed, at Mrs Bannister's request, to help with passing round food and organizing the games Lilly wanted to play with her friends – and it was as well that he did. He had to use Ctrl-Z three times that afternoon: once when

Callum accidentally spilt a jug of Ribena on to the sound system Mr Bannister had set up; once when he tripped on a tree root, dropping a tray of cutlery on to the head of one of Lilly's friends; and a third time when he set fire to the sitting room.

The fire happened when Callum's mother asked him to tie up Mojo so that he didn't bother the guests, some of whom were rather nervous of a large dog bounding round the garden. Callum tied him to the barbecue, which was all right until Mojo decided to drag himself (and the barbecue) indoors and set light to the sitting-room curtains. Happily, on all three occasions, Alex was able to go back to before the accidents had happened and make sure that they didn't.

'We're so grateful to you!' Mrs Bannister told him when Lilly had been sent indoors to rest and Alex was about to go home. 'It's been the most wonderful afternoon and we couldn't have done it without you.'

'Me?' Alex wondered for a moment if Callum had told her about his computer. 'I didn't do anything . . . really.'

'Oh yes, you did.' Mrs Bannister beamed down at him. 'I saw the way you kept watching Callum, making sure that nothing happened that could spoil everything, and nothing did! We're very grateful to you!'

She gave him a large piece of cake and a giant bottle of fizzy orange and, as Alex walked home with his laptop tucked under his arm, he was filled with the sense that it had been a good day.

A very good day.

Turning into the drive that led up to his own house, his mother lifted her head from under the bonnet of her car and asked how the party had been.

'It was brilliant,' said Alex. 'Lilly had a really good time.'

'That's nice . . .' Alex's mother held up a spark plug and examined it carefully. For two years now she had been doing up an old Triumph TR4, and although the work was almost finished, the engine still didn't run as smoothly as she'd like. 'And how many accidents did Callum have?'

'None,' said Alex. 'He didn't have any.'

'That must be a first.' Mrs Howard was checking the gap in the plug with a micron gauge, but then peered over the top of the car at Alex. 'You're not hungry or anything, are you? Only I'd quite like to finish this.'

Alex said he had had plenty to eat at the party and went indoors. He got himself a glass from the kitchen and took it with the fizzy orange and the computer upstairs to his room.

Walking home from the Bannisters', he had had

an idea. If he set the clock on the laptop for a time later in the day rather than earlier, maybe Ctrl-Z could send him forward to a time in the future, instead of the past. He could think of several ways this might be useful. If you were going to the dentist, say, or didn't want to do some homework, skipping forward to after it had happened and missing out all the uncomfortable bits would be kind of neat.

Disappointingly, when he tried it, nothing happened. Sitting at the desk in his bedroom, he typed in a time thirty minutes in the future and pressed Ctrl-Z, but instead of finding himself doing whatever he would be doing in half an hour, the time on the computer simply returned to what it had been before and Alex remained firmly in the present.

He was equally unsuccessful when he tried changing the date. He thought it might be fun to move to a different day in the future or the past, but quickly discovered that the date, like his name, could not be altered. The only thing he could change was the time on the clock to something earlier.

He drank his fizzy orange and wondered why this should be. It was only one of a growing list of questions to which he wanted to know the answer. Like what happened to the times that no

27

longer existed because he had gone back and changed them? What, for instance, happened to the time when the balloons had floated off with the garden chair? Where did it go?

The only person he knew who might be able to tell him was Godfather John, and Alex was wondering about the best way to contact him when he heard the sound of his parents' voices in the kitchen downstairs.

The voices were raised and he realized, with a sinking feeling, that they were arguing.

Again.

Alex could remember a time when his parents never argued at all. In fact, for most of his life he could hardly remember them even getting upset. Other children might have parents who quarrelled, got angry and shouted at each other, but life at number 17 Oakwood Close had always been remarkably quiet and peaceful.

And then, a few months before, they had started having these arguments – not all the time, just occasionally and about the silliest things. They argued about who hadn't hung up a bath towel, or who hadn't turned off a light, and they had even had one argument that lasted over an hour about whether a screwdriver had been put back in the right drawer in the utility room.

Alex crept out on to the landing so that he could

hear what they were saying and found that this time they seemed to be arguing about supper.

'You were the one who suggested it.' His father's voice came up from the kitchen. 'You were the one who said you wanted to cook a proper meal.'

'I'm sorry!' said his mother. 'I was working on the car and I forgot.'

'Oh yes, your car!' Mr Howard sounded thoroughly aggrieved. 'I can see that was *so* much more important . . .'

'Oh, for heaven's sake!' said Mrs Howard. 'If you're hungry I can still make you something. Just give me half an hour!'

'I don't have half an hour,' said Mr Howard. 'I have to leave by then.'

'So I'll make you a sandwich! It's not the end of the world.'

'If I wanted a sandwich,' said Mr Howard, 'I could buy one at a garage. In fact, I think that's what I'll do.'

Alex could hear his father's steps in the hall.

'Oh, for goodness' sake, Steven! There's no need to –' Mrs Howard tried calling after her husband, but it was too late. There was the sound of the front door slamming and Mr Howard was gone. Alex could hear his mother in the kitchen muttering and then the noise of her banging something against the wall. It sounded like it might be her head.

He thought for a moment, then went back into his room and reached for the laptop on his desk.

'How was the party?' asked his mother, lifting her head from the bonnet of her car as Alex came up the drive.

'It was brilliant,' said Alex. 'Lilly had a really good time.'

'That's nice . . .' Alex's mother held up a spark plug and examined it carefully. 'And how many accidents did Callum have?'

'None,' said Alex. 'Are we having supper soon?'

'Supper?' Mrs Howard looked up from measuring the gap in the spark plug with a micron gauge. 'Didn't you eat at the party?'

'Yes,' said Alex, 'but I thought Dad said something about you cooking a proper meal this evening.'

'What?' His mother looked blankly at him for a moment and then her eyes widened. 'Oh goodness! So I am!' She began wiping her hands on a rag and then pulling off the boiler suit she wore for working on the car. 'I meant to tell you. He's got to drive to Nottingham tonight and tomorrow he's speaking at a conference. I thought a nice supper might cheer him up.' She put a hand on Alex's shoulder. 'You don't mind, do you?'

'No,' said Alex. 'No, that's fine.'

It was a very pleasant meal. Mrs Howard had

made spaghetti and while they ate Mr Howard explained to Alex why he hoped going to Nottingham would provide some useful contacts for his work. Mrs Howard told Mr Howard how she had sorted out the ignition timing problem on her car, and Alex told them both about Lilly's coming home party and the hundred balloons tied up around the garden.

Afterwards, when Alex went out to see his father off, his father took him to one side and asked him to take care of his mother until he got back on Tuesday. 'She's under a lot of pressure at the moment,' he said, 'with all these job interviews and applications.'

At the moment, Alex's mother worked as the receptionist at a garage, but for some years she had been taking the exams that would let her get a job as an accountant.

'Look after her, will you?' said Mr Howard.

And Alex promised that he would.

After his father had left, Alex took his computer to the bench at the bottom of the garden and sat there in the evening sun. He was feeling rather pleased with himself and not even the noise of Mr Kowalski next door shouting at a cat that had got into his garden could disturb his mood.

He opened the laptop and while he waited for

the machine to load up, wondered exactly what he was going to say.

Godfather John was not an easy man to contact. He had an address – somewhere in Australia – and a phone number, but if you tried to write or call, you might not get a reply for weeks. According to Alex's father, Godfather John's lifestyle was as unusual as the presents he sent and he spent a lot of his time travelling. Occasionally these travels had meant calling in at Oakwood Close, but this had not happened recently and Alex hadn't actually seen his godfather since he was five.

But it didn't matter if he couldn't telephone or write a letter, Alex thought, because now he could use his laptop to send an email. With the computer open on his lap, he clicked on the icon that brought up the email from Godfather John and pressed Reply.

Dear Godfather John, he wrote,
Thank you for the birthday present you sent me. It is brilliant. I have had such a good day. If anything bad happens all I have to do is press Ctrl-Z and I go back and change it. It is so cool!

He went on to describe what had happened when the parcel arrived and then how he had used the computer at Callum's house. He didn't mention the row his parents had been having, though, and instead, at the end, he wrote –

Can I ask where you got it from? And how it was made and how it works? And I was wondering what happens to all the times that don't happen because I have gone back and changed them? If nobody else remembers them, did they ever happen at all?
It really is the best present ever!
Love
Alex

When he had finished, he pressed the Send button, then sat back as the laptop connected itself to the wireless router in the house and the message disappeared.

He leant back on the bench and stared up at the sky. The sun had set and the first stars were faintly visible, but Alex didn't see them.

His mind was too busy wondering what he might do with Ctrl-Z tomorrow.

CHAPTER FOUR

The next morning, when Alex woke up, the first thing he did was go over to his desk and turn on his laptop. He set the time for two minutes earlier, pressed Ctrl-Z, and found himself back in bed looking up at the ceiling.

He lay there for a moment contentedly. It hadn't been a dream! With Ctrl-Z, he really could send himself back to any point in the day, and the night before he had worked out two things that he particularly wanted to do with this new ability.

The first of them was very simple. He was going to go next door and get back his cricket ball. He had lost it over the fence two evenings before – in the last month he had also lost three tennis balls and a frisbee – but had never dared to try to get it back.

The old man at number 16 was not an easy neighbour. Mr Kowalski lived alone and hated any dogs, cats or children coming into his garden. He had actually run lengths of barbed wire along the top of the fence to keep them out and Alex had decided some time ago that the only thing to do when you lost a ball over the fence to number 16 was forget about it and buy a new one.

However, with Ctrl-Z, the situation was different. It was one thing to creep into Mr Kowalski's garden to look for a cricket ball when Mr Kowalski might burst out of his house at any moment and catch you, but quite another to go there knowing that if he did appear, you could get yourself out of trouble at the touch of a button. If Alex was carrying the computer, it wouldn't matter if Mr Kowalski came out. All he would have to do was press Ctrl-Z and he would be safely back in his bedroom deciding whether or not he wanted to go.

An hour later, with his laptop balanced on one arm and the time on it set for ten minutes earlier, Alex strode confidently down the path at the side of Mr Kowalski's house and into his back garden. The old man was indoors and, as all the windows of his house were tightly closed and the curtains drawn – they always were, no one knew why – there was no reason why he should know Alex was there.

He searched the garden thoroughly – twice – but without finding his cricket ball. He checked over the vegetable patch, walked up and down the flower beds and scanned every inch of the lawn, but there was no sign of it. Or of his frisbee, or any of the tennis balls. Disappointed, he was just double-checking one of the flower beds before leaving when –

'Get away! You are *very* bad! Get away!'

The sound of Mr Kowalski's voice was so sudden and so startling that Alex dropped his computer. It landed on the grass at his feet and, as he bent down to retrieve it, he realized two things. One was that Mr Kowalski was not shouting at *him* in his heavy Polish accent, but at a small white dog, which had been sniffing around the vegetable patch and was now running for its life. The second was that Mr Kowalski had a gun.

'You don't stay away, I shoot you!' Mr Kowalski shouted and, pointing the gun at the dog as it raced across the garden, fired twice. The *ping* of pellets bouncing off the fence at least told Alex it was only an air pistol, but any reassurance he might have felt disappeared as Mr Kowalski turned and saw him.

'Alex?' he demanded sharply. 'What you doing? What you doing in my garden?'

'I-I –' Praying that the computer had survived

the fall, Alex lifted his hand, pushed down on Ctrl-Z and found himself back in his bedroom, quite unharmed, but with his heart thumping heavily in his chest.

His first idea may not have been as successful as he'd hoped, but it didn't really matter, Alex thought. It was his second idea that was the exciting one and, after telling his mother where he was going, he walked down the road to talk it over with Callum.

Callum, however, was not at home. Alex rang the doorbell several times without getting an answer before Mrs Penrose came out of the house next door to tell him that the Bannisters had all gone off in a car about half an hour earlier. Alex asked if she knew when they would be back – Mrs Penrose usually knew everything like that about her neighbours – but on this occasion she didn't.

'I would have asked them,' she said, 'but I was a bit upset at the time. About Jennings.'

'Jennings?'

'My dog,' Mrs Penrose explained. 'He's small, white . . . You haven't seen him, have you?'

Alex wondered if he should say he had seen it in Mr Kowalski's garden being shot at, but decided against it. Mrs Penrose had already lost one dog that year, and if she'd lost another he didn't want to be the one to break the news.

He called back twice in the next couple of hours, but Callum had not returned and he still wasn't back at half past one when Alex and his mother left for the fête. Which was a shame because that was where Alex was planning to put his second idea into practice.

The school fête was held on the playing field every year in the middle of May, and Alex and Callum normally went to it together. This year, however, the fête was almost over and Mr Eccles the head teacher had finished giving out the prizes for the Grand Draw before Callum finally turned up. When he did arrive, he was wearing a neck-brace and could speak only in a hoarse whisper.

Alex asked what had happened.

'He's lucky to be alive,' said Mrs Bannister. 'He nearly strangled himself this morning.'

'Strangled himself?' said Alex. 'How?'

'I had an accident,' whispered Callum hoarsely. 'With Dad's paper shredder.'

Alex wasn't quite sure how even Callum could strangle himself with a paper shredder, but it turned out he had got his pyjama top caught in the machine while he was using it; the cloth had been pulled through with such force that the material had tightened round his neck and almost throttled him. Mr Bannister had found him and cut him free just in time.

'You should see the bruises on his neck,' said Mrs Bannister. 'And the doctor says he's torn four separate muscles and needs to wear the neck-brace for a month.' She sighed. 'We were six hours in Casualty while they fitted it. That's why we're late.'

'Why didn't you call me?' demanded Alex as Mrs Bannister went off to the tea tent. 'So I could sort things out.'

'What do you mean?' croaked Callum.

'I told you yesterday,' said Alex. 'Anything happens, any time you have an accident, all you have to do is let me know and I can go back in time so that it doesn't happen. I *told* you!'

'Did you?' Callum frowned. 'When?'

'Yesterday! I told you just after –' Alex was about to say that he had told Callum just after he had sat on Lilly's present, when he remembered that he had used Ctrl-Z to go back before that time, so Callum wouldn't remember.

'But you do remember I told you about Ctrl-Z?'

'Oh yes . . .' Callum looked slightly embarrassed. 'I remember that, but . . .'

'OK!' Alex held up his hand. 'We'll go over it

later. First things first. When did the accident happen?'

'This morning.'

'No, no, I need to know exactly,' said Alex. 'What time was it?'

After some thought, Callum decided it must have been about quarter past nine.

'Quarter past nine? You're sure?'

'I think so. What . . . Where are you going?'

Alex was already on his feet. 'Home,' he said. 'And then back to this morning, to make sure you don't do anything stupid with a shredder.'

To be on the safe side, Alex went back to nine o'clock, and found himself in his bedroom that morning. A few minutes later he was ringing the bell at the Bannisters' house and Callum answered the door, dressed in his pyjamas.

'I've come to warn you about using the shredder,' said Alex.

Callum looked at him blankly. 'What?'

'You've got to be careful using the shredder,' said Alex, 'because if you get your pyjama top caught in it, you'll strangle yourself.'

'I've never used a shredder in my life,' said Callum. 'Why would I use a shredder? I haven't got anything to shred.'

At that moment, Mr Bannister came out of the

dining room with a sheaf of papers in one hand, which he passed to Callum.

'Put these through the shredder for me, will you, Callum?' he said. 'I've got to make some phone calls and I have to be out of the house in five minutes.' He gave Alex a cheery wave and disappeared into the kitchen.

Callum stared at the sheaf of papers in his hand and then at Alex. 'How . . . How did you know that . . . ?'

Alex sighed and wondered how many more times he would have to explain it to Callum before he understood.

'Just do the shredding,' he said, 'and I'll tell you.'

While Callum did the shredding, Alex explained how he had already spent the day – what had happened with Mr Kowalski, how he had gone to the fête, and how Callum had appeared with a neck-brace – then finally how he had gone back to the start of it to make sure the accident didn't happen.

At the end, Callum sat there, nodding slowly.

'So in future,' Alex finished up, 'any time anything bad happens to you, you have to tell me about it, straight away. OK?'

'Because you can go back and stop it happening?' said Callum.

'Right,' said Alex. He sat down on the floor beside his friend. 'Now, I'll tell you what's going to happen this afternoon . . .'

At the fête that afternoon, Alex was finally able to put the second of his ideas into practice. He began at a small table near the entrance where his form teacher, Miss Simpson, stood behind a large jar of Smarties. If you guessed how many Smarties there were, said the sign along the front, then you could win the whole jar.

Alex consulted a piece of paper he had taken from his pocket. 'It's six thousand, three hundred and ninety-four,' he said.

'You're sure?' asked Callum.

'Positive,' said Alex confidently. 'I've done all this before, remember?'

Alex had already seen the prize jar of Smarties being awarded and been careful to make a note of the winning number. He had written it down – then written down the location of the square in which the £20 note was buried in the Treasure Hunt, the combination on the padlock to the bottle of champagne, and all the numbers on the winning tickets in the Grand Draw.

He didn't have that piece of paper with him now, of course, because as soon as he had gone home and pressed Ctrl-Z, he had gone back to before he had written it. However, the last thing he had done before pressing the keys on his computer, had been to go over the numbers several times in his head, and the first thing he had done when he found himself back at nine o'clock in the morning was write them all down again before he forgot. They were listed on the piece of paper he now held in his hand.

'Come on.' Alex led Callum across the grass to the Treasure Hunt. 'We'll do the twenty-pound note next.'

After the Smarties, the Treasure Hunt and the champagne, Alex moved on to buying raffle tickets. He bought the winning numbers for a flat-screen television, a hamper of groceries, the use of a cottage in Cornwall for a week in August, an oil painting of a sunset and seven other smaller items.

'You're going to win them all!' said Callum excitedly. 'You're going to win everything!'

'And that's only the beginning,' Alex agreed happily. 'Next Saturday, I'm going to do the lottery.'

'The lottery?'

'Think about it,' said Alex. 'All I have to do is wait till they've announced the winning numbers, use Ctrl-Z to go back to earlier in the day, then buy the ticket. I can't lose!'

For a moment, neither of them said anything as they considered what this meant.

'The week after,' said Alex, 'I could give you the winning numbers, if you like.'

Callum said he'd like that very much, but pointed out that you have to be over sixteen before you are allowed to buy a lottery ticket.

They were still discussing the best way to get round this when the tannoy system announced that the prize-giving was about to start.

When Mr Eccles the head teacher said that Alex had won the jar of Smarties by guessing the exact number inside, there was a big cheer from the assembled parents and children as he went up to collect it.

When it was revealed that he had also guessed the magic square in the Treasure Hunt, there was another round of applause and some laughter as he went up to collect the twenty-pound note as well. There was rather less applause when he won the bottle of champagne and, as he went up to collect the hairdryer, the first of the prizes in the Grand Draw, most people were not clapping at all.

That was when Alex realized he might have made a mistake.

'They don't like it, do they?' said Callum, as Alex came back with the hairdryer. 'When you win everything, I mean.'

And he was right. By now there were hostile murmurings from several parts of the crowd. A girl from Alex's class called Sophie Reynolds said in a loud voice that she thought he was cheating, but he didn't know what he could do. He wondered about going to the tea tent to find his mother or Mrs Bannister. He wondered about quietly throwing away his tickets and pretending he hadn't bought them, and he wondered about simply running away . . .

He was still wondering when Mr Eccles, after giving the box of draw tickets a particularly vigorous shake and getting a small girl in the front row to pick out a ticket, announced that the winner of the hamper of groceries was ticket 576.

'It's the wrong number!' Callum shuffled through the tickets they had bought and then looked at Alex's list. 'It was supposed to be three hundred and seventy-three!'

Alex was the one who worked out what had happened. The number was different because Mr Eccles was behaving differently. When he had watched the prize-giving the first time, Alex remembered, Mr Eccles had picked out all the numbers himself. He had not given the box a particularly hard shake, nor had he asked a girl from the front row of the crowd to choose a ticket. He was behaving differently this time so naturally the numbers that were chosen in the draw would be different as well.

It was, if he was honest, something of a relief. He had the definite feeling that if he had won anything else, the crowd would have done more than just mutter.

All in all, it was a disappointing afternoon, and it wasn't made any better when he dropped the jar of Smarties in a gutter on the way home and then found, two minutes later, that the twenty-pound note had fallen through a hole in his pocket. By the time he had given the hairdryer to his mother and the bottle of champagne to Mrs Bannister it meant he had no prizes at all.

'Never mind.' Callum put a hand on his shoulder. 'You can still do the lottery on Saturday.'

But it turned out Callum was wrong. When he got home from the fête and went up to his room, Alex found an email on his computer from Godfather John, which said –

Dear Alex

Thank you for your letter, and it was good to hear you were enjoying Ctrl-Z. How interesting that you should have started off by using it to stop your friend having quite so many accidents – and how kind – though I am sure you will soon discover it is only one of a good many things you can do!

And perhaps I should have warned you about one of them. It will probably occur to you at some point that you can use Ctrl-Z to put a bet on a horse race, play the Stock Exchange or win the National Lottery – and I'm afraid, if you do, the results will be disappointing. Ctrl-Z will not allow you to violate the Universal Law of Appropriate Returns and you will find, if you try it, that you never get the reward you expected. My advice is to give all those things a miss.

However, if you give the matter some thought, I'm sure you will soon realize there are at least twenty-seven legitimate means of making money with Ctrl-Z, any of which will have much happier results.

So have fun, make mistakes, and if you have a chance to tell me about them, do write again!

Your loving godfather

John Presley

PS In answer to your question 'Where did you get Ctrl-Z?', I made it myself. How I made it and how it works is rather more complicated and an explanation may have to wait until you have a basic grasp of quantum physics. In the meantime, however, I suggest you just sit back and enjoy it!

When he had read the letter, Alex leant back in his chair and stared thoughtfully at the computer screen. He had never heard of the Universal Law of Appropriate Returns, but it might explain his dropping the jar of Smarties into a gutter and then losing the twenty-pound note through a hole in his pocket. They were the sort of accidents that Callum might have had, but not Alex. If his uncle was right, he thought, it meant there would be no millions from the lottery. Which was a shame.

Though the idea that there were twenty-seven ways he *could* use Ctrl-Z to make money legitimately was encouraging.

He wondered what they might be.

CHAPTER FIVE

'Twenty-seven?' said Callum as he and Alex were walking to school the next morning. 'Twenty-seven ways to make money?'

'At *least* twenty-seven,' said Alex. 'That's what he said in the email.'

Callum frowned. 'Like what?'

So far, Alex had to admit, he didn't know. He had lain in bed the night before for over an hour, trying to think of even one way that Ctrl-Z could be used to make money and come up with nothing. He had rather hoped that Callum might be able to help.

'Sorry,' said Callum, after considering the problem for several minutes. 'I can't think of anything.'

It wasn't important, Alex thought. They had plenty of time to work on it and, in the meantime, he had had an idea how his computer might be useful at school.

'I was thinking of using it in the test this morning,' he said.

Each Monday morning, Miss Simpson gave her class a general knowledge test based on events that had been on the news or in the papers over the weekend. The person who got the most marks could choose a sweet from the treats jar and most weeks it was Sophie Reynolds, who always seemed to know everything. As a rule, neither Alex nor Callum did particularly well.

'But if I listen to the answers,' Alex explained, 'then go back to before the test started and take it again, I should be able to get full marks, shouldn't I!'

'Yes . . .' Callum agreed cautiously, 'except you don't have the computer with you, do you?'

He could see Alex was only carrying his school bag, and there wasn't room in it for his laptop.

Alex had thought about taking his computer to school, but decided in the end that it would not be wise. You were not supposed to bring anything that ran on batteries on to school premises and if you did, Mr Eccles was liable to confiscate it. His computer would be useful in school, Alex knew, but nothing was worth the risk of losing it.

'It doesn't make any difference, though,' he told Callum, 'because I just have to wait till I get home, don't I? Then I can use it to go back to whenever I want.'

'If you did that,' said Callum, 'it would mean sitting through all the lessons again. Even Geography.'

This was, Alex had to admit, a serious consideration. Geography was boring enough the first time round. No one would go through it twice without a very good reason. A better reason than a free sweet, anyway.

'OK,' he said, 'maybe I'll save the test idea for another time.'

But when they got to school, Callum had another of his accidents.

At the fête the day before, Callum had bought a pot of something called Roller Putty. It was odd stuff, slightly sticky, but when rolled in a ball, bounced off the walls or the floor with extraordinary speed. He was giving a demonstration of this in the boys' toilets before school started and threw the Roller Putty on to the floor, where it bounced straight up to the ceiling above one of the lavatories . . . and stuck there.

Callum climbed on to the lavatory bowl to get it back, but slipped. His right foot landed in the bowl and he couldn't get it out. He pulled and twisted, but however hard he tried, his foot was firmly jammed down the bend in the pan.

'Don't panic,' said Alex. 'I'll get Mr Boney.'

Mr Boney was the school caretaker and while waiting for him to arrive Callum struggled desperately to get free, and – and this was his real mistake – grabbed hold of the cistern on the wall above the toilet to try to get some leverage to pull his foot out. As he tugged, the cistern came away from the wall.

There was a lot of water. There was the water from the cistern, which emptied itself down Callum's front, there was more water flushing up his trouser leg from the bowl and there was a huge amount of water spraying on to his face and chest from the broken pipe on the wall.

It took the caretaker fifteen minutes to turn off the water and get Callum's foot free from the toilet, by which time the entire room was flooded. Then Callum had to report to Mr Eccles the head teacher, who lectured him on the cost of damage done to school property by carelessness, before sending him to get some dry clothes from the office.

The school office kept a small supply of clothes that students could borrow in an emergency. Most of them, however, were for younger children and the best that the secretary could offer Callum was a pair of rather small PE shorts and a girl's blouse. On top of what had already happened it was, to say the least, embarrassing.

'Goodness, Callum!' said Miss Simpson when he finally arrived at the classroom. 'What happened to you?'

'He had an accident in the toilets, Miss,' said Sophie Reynolds.

'Well, never mind!' Miss Simpson patted Callum's shoulder sympathetically. 'A lot of children have that problem and I'm sure you'll grow out of it.'

Callum wanted to explain it had not been that sort of accident but Miss Simpson was already telling everyone to get out their pens for the general knowledge test.

For both boys, the test was even worse than usual. Alex got one right answer out of twenty and Callum got none at all. The sweet from the treats jar went to Sophie Reynolds again, and at break time the two boys sat on a bench in the playground feeling rather depressed.

On top of the accident and the test, Alex had just discovered he had forgotten to pack his lunch box in his bag, and Callum had found out that Sophie Reynolds had somehow taken a video of him with his foot in the toilet on her mobile phone and was going to post it that evening on the Internet. He had pleaded with her not to do this, but Sophie had told him that if he had been someone she liked she might have agreed, but he wasn't.

'It'll be OK,' Alex told him. 'When I get home, I'll be able to make all this not happen.'

'Yes,' said Callum. 'That'll be good.' But it didn't sound like the idea cheered him up much.

'You don't need to worry about it.'

'No.'

'We just have to wait, that's all.'

Callum nodded, but he wasn't happy. Even if Alex could make everything all right eventually, somehow he still had to get through the rest of the day.

Then, as he was walking back to class at the end of break, Alex suddenly realized he *didn't* have to wait till the end of the day before going home and pressing Ctrl-Z on his computer. He could go home now. And there was no need to worry about getting into trouble for leaving school without permission because by the time he'd got home and pressed Ctrl-Z, no one would know that that was what he had done. In fact, he wouldn't have done it. That was the whole point. None of the events of the morning would have happened.

Instead of going to the classroom, he made his way down the corridor that led to the main entrance . . . then stopped at the supply cupboard outside the library. The door was open and the sight of the contents inside gave him an idea.

Thoughtfully, he reached up to one of the shelves and took down a bucket of wallpaper paste that had been put there for the Year Ones to use to make papier mâché masks. Before he went home, he thought, there was one thing he wanted to do . . .

In the classroom, Miss Simpson had begun flashing up pictures of a farm in Brazil on the whiteboard and didn't see Alex as he came in, walked straight over to the table by the window and carefully emptied the bucket of paste over Sophie Reynolds's head. Sophie screamed, there was a gasp from the class and Miss Simpson, when she turned round and saw what had happened, was at first too astonished to speak. For several seconds the entire class sat there in silence staring at Alex and the only sound was the drip of wallpaper paste as it slid down Sophie's face and on to the floor.

'If anyone's wondering why I did that,' said Alex, 'I'll tell you. I don't like Sophie. Yesterday she said I was cheating when I won a prize at the fête, and this morning she took photos of Callum when he got his foot stuck in the toilet and said she's going to put them on the web. I thought she deserved to have something bad happen to her for a change.'

'Alex Howard!' Miss Simpson had finally recovered her voice. 'Have you gone completely mad?'

'It's all right,' said Alex. 'No need to get upset.' He smiled. 'You'll want me to go to Mr Eccles's office now, I expect.' Despite what had happened, he felt remarkably calm. 'I'll go and do that then, shall I?'

He left the classroom and walked along the corridor to the Head's office. He didn't go in, though. Instead, he went straight past to where the school receptionist was at her desk and tapped on the window.

'Mr Eccles says can he have a jug of hot water, please,' he said.

'A jug of hot water?' The receptionist looked puzzled. 'What for?'

Alex gave a shrug. 'He just said to ask if you could bring it to his office.'

With a sigh, the receptionist got up and disappeared in the direction of the kitchens. As soon as she was out of sight, Alex pressed the security button that unlocked the front door and walked out. The path that led to the road was screened by bushes so nobody saw him as he strode out through the school gates and began walking home.

He didn't have his bag with him – that was still in the classroom – but it didn't matter because when he pressed Ctrl-Z the bag would be with him at home again. Nothing mattered. It was a warm day and, as he walked, he took off his sweatshirt and left it hanging on some railings. There was no point in carrying it if he didn't need it. That was something else that didn't matter.

If anyone had stopped him on the way home and asked why he wasn't in school, he had a story ready about being off with suspected measles, but nobody did. Nobody gave him a second glance and he was back in Oakwood Close fifteen minutes later, collecting the spare key from under the loose brick in the paving so that he could open the front door.

The only person who saw him was Mr Kowalski, who was out in his front garden planting some geraniums. He was wearing the grey cardigan with the holes in the elbows that he always wore, and there was a stubble of unshaven hairs on his chin.

'Hey, Alex!' he called. 'Why you not in school?', but Alex didn't answer. He simply smiled and waved, and let himself indoors.

The house was empty. His mother and father

were both at work and Alex helped himself to a can of drink and a chocolate bar from the tin in the kitchen. Normally he was only allowed a chocolate bar if he asked his parents first, but today there was no need to ask anybody about anything because very soon this, like everything else, would never have happened.

He watched some television while he finished his drink and ate the chocolate bar, then made his way upstairs to his room. Sitting at his desk, he opened his laptop, set the time for twenty-five past eight in the morning and pressed Ctrl-Z.

An instant later, he was walking along the pavement with Callum.

'Twenty-seven?' Callum was saying. 'Twenty-seven ways to make money?'

'At *least* twenty-seven,' said Alex, 'and before you ask what any of them are, I have to go back and get my lunch box, and then I'm going to warn you about the Roller Putty . . .'

The second time around, the morning was much more pleasant. On the walk to school, Alex went over the questions he could remember from Miss Simpson's general knowledge test and both boys did rather well. Sophie Reynolds tried not to show it, but you could see she was distinctly put out at coming third.

It was, from everyone else's point of view, a very ordinary day, but Alex found himself thinking at odd moments how different it had been the first time around. He thought about pouring the bucket of paste over Sophie Reynolds's head and how calm he had felt as he offered to report himself to the head teacher. He thought about what it had been like to walk out of school in the middle of the morning and to leave all his cares, like his school sweatshirt, hanging on some railings behind him.

He was finally beginning to realize that, with Ctrl-Z, you could do anything. Anything at all. Whatever you wanted, however strange or dangerous or wicked – however much trouble it would cause – you could just go ahead and do it.

And *that* was an idea with some interesting possibilities.

CHAPTER SIX

'You're going to what?' asked Callum.

'I'm going to borrow Mum's car and take it for a drive,' Alex repeated.

He and Callum were standing in the garage to one side of Mrs Howard's precious TR4. It was Tuesday, they had just got back from school and Alex had everything worked out. He had collected the keys from the hook by the back door in the kitchen, his mother would not be cycling home from her work at the garage for another half-hour and he was ready to go.

'But you can't!' There was a look of panic on Callum's face. 'Your mum's spent years doing that thing up; if you damage it . . .'

'You still don't get it, do you?' said Alex. 'It doesn't *matter* if I damage it. Because when you

60

press Ctrl-Z, none of this is ever going to have happened.'

'Me?' Callum's look of panic deepened. '*I'm* going to press Ctrl-Z?'

'Well, I can't do it, can I!' Alex passed him the computer. 'I'm going to have both hands busy with the steering.' He pulled open the car door. 'I've set the time. All you have to do is press Ctrl-Z when I tell you.'

Sitting in the car, he adjusted the seat, put the key into the ignition and turned it. There was a throaty roar from the engine and Alex smiled happily to himself. All he had to do now was depress the clutch and put the gear stick into reverse. He had seen his mother do it a thousand times . . .

'Please, Alex!' Callum's anxious face appeared alongside him. 'Don't do this! If something happens –'

'Nothing's going to happen,' Alex waved him away. 'And don't press Ctrl-Z till I say!'

There was a grinding noise as he put the car into gear then, as he took his foot off the clutch, the car leapt backwards rather faster than he'd expected. The side of the car scraped along the edge of the garage and the wing mirror *pinged* off on to the floor. Alex hurtled down the drive, pulled hard on the steering wheel, swung the car round and ran straight along the pavement into a lamp post.

The car stalled, and when he turned the ignition again, nothing happened.

'OK!' He called back to the open-mouthed Callum. 'You can press it now!'

Alex had six more goes with the car and by the last attempt felt he was really getting the hang of it. He could reverse out of the drive without hitting the side of the garage or crashing into the lamp post. He could change into a forward gear without stalling, and got all the way to the end of the road, turned round, came back and into his own drive before stopping in front of a white-faced Callum and telling him to press Ctrl-Z.

An instant later, he was no longer in the car, but standing to one side of it in the garage.

'You're going to *what*?' demanded Callum.

'I said I'm going to borrow Mum's car and take it for a drive,' said Alex, but then decided he had done enough driving for one day. 'No, on second thoughts, let's go and have some tea.'

'Thank goodness for that.' Callum gave a sigh of relief. 'Your mum's spent years doing up the car and if anything happened to it . . .'

'Come on.' Alex took his friend by the arm and led him towards the road. 'Let's get to your house and I'll tell you what just happened.'

★

The next day, when he got home from school, Alex took the 120-piece dinner service his parents had been given when they got married – the one they only used when they had special visitors – and carried it out to the garden. Standing by the back door, he picked up one of the dinner plates and hurled it like a discus as far as he could. It landed with a deeply satisfying crash on the paving stones down by the shed.

Ten plates later, Callum was finally persuaded to join in, and he threw a soup plate, which unfortunately went over the fence into the garden next door, breaking not only the plate but a pane of glass in Mr Kowalski's greenhouse. That made an even better noise, Alex decided, and he began throwing more china over the fence directly at the greenhouse.

Five minutes later, when every single piece of china had been shattered – and most of the greenhouse – Alex gazed happily at the wreckage and not even the sudden appearance of Mr Kowalski's unshaven face above the fence could disturb his feeling of deep content.

'Alex?' bellowed Mr Kowalski. 'What you done? What you done to my greenhouse!' His finger pointed accusingly. 'You are wicked boy! I tell your father! You are very wicked boy!'

While Callum backed nervously towards the

house, Alex did not bat an eyelid. 'Don't worry, Mr K,' he said calmly. 'It's cool.'

And it *was* cool. Everything was always cool when you had Ctrl-Z, that was the point. You never had to worry about what might go wrong and, in a way, that feeling was even better than the fun of taking your mother's car for a drive or smashing a greenhouse with Royal Doulton china.

Throughout his entire life Alex had been told what he could do, what he couldn't, and how important it was to follow certain rules. Now, suddenly, for a part of the day at least, there were no rules. He could do anything. He could do whatever he wanted. He had to go back afterwards and *not* do it, of course, but for a while he was completely free. It was one of the best feelings he had ever had.

In the days that followed, Alex did a good many of the things that would, under normal circumstances, have got him into a great deal of trouble. He pulled out the bottom cans from the pyramid displays of baked beans at the supermarket, he dropped a television from the top of a multi-storey car park, and he even managed, on a brief train journey to Oxford, to pull the lever that told the driver to make an emergency stop.

To be honest, not all the things he did were

quite as much fun as he had hoped, and one of them – setting off a fire extinguisher in a shopping mall, turned out to be no fun at all.

It should have been. The idea was simple enough. It was the weekend, and Mrs Bannister had taken the boys into town and left them at the cafe in the middle of the mall with a bun and a Coca-Cola, while she went off to pick up some medicine for Lilly from the chemist.

The fire extinguisher was sitting invitingly in a corner with the instructions on how to work it written clearly on its side. Alex had his laptop with him in his backpack and setting it off seemed like a fun thing to do.

Callum had the job of standing with his fingers poised, ready to press Ctrl-Z as soon as anyone in authority appeared, and it was only when Alex had actually picked up the extinguisher that he saw, walking towards them, Sophie Reynolds.

'You should aim the nozzle at her,' said Callum. 'It'd be much funnier than just splashing the stuff on the floor.'

Spraying someone you didn't like very much with chemical foam seemed a brilliant idea. Alex pulled the handle on the extinguisher and a wonderful white spray poured out of the nozzle. In seconds Sophie was covered from head to toe, but she didn't scream this time as she had done with the wallpaper paste. Instead, she simply stood there, and then her face crumpled and she began to cry.

That was when the idea didn't seem quite so funny.

A moment later, a woman in a wheelchair appeared beside Sophie. Oddly, she was the only one of the people passing by who seemed to take any notice of what had happened and she held Sophie's hand and looked rather upset.

'Sophie?' she said anxiously. 'Sophie, darling, are you all right? What's happened?' She turned in her wheelchair towards Alex and her voice was more puzzled than anything else. 'Why?' she asked. 'Why did you do that?'

That was when the idea didn't seem funny at all, and the two seconds before Callum remembered to stop staring and press Ctrl-Z, felt like a lifetime.

'You should aim the nozzle at her,' said Callum. 'It'd be much funnier than just splashing the stuff on the floor.'

'No,' said Alex slowly, 'I don't think that's a good idea.'

'Why not?' Callum insisted. 'We don't like her! She's always showing off in class and –' He stopped. Sophie was standing directly in front of them.

'Hi,' she said.

'Hi,' said Alex.

'Look . . . um . . .' Sophie was blushing slightly. 'I need some help. With my mum.' She pointed over her shoulder to a woman in a wheelchair approaching them. 'We've got a problem with the wheelchair.'

'What sort of problem?' asked Alex.

'We can't get it up the ramp,' said Sophie. 'With all the shopping, it's too heavy. I'm not strong enough.'

'Yes, of course,' said Alex. He was already moving towards Sophie's mother. 'We're experts at moving wheelchairs. Callum's sister is in one at the moment.'

'Is she?' Sophie looked at Callum in surprise. 'I didn't know that. Why?'

On their way to the ramps that led up to the car park, Callum explained about his sister and her osteomyelitis, and Sophie's mother explained about the accident that had left her unable to move below the waist. Apparently it meant that Sophie had to do a lot of the housework and Mrs Reynolds said she wished sometimes that her daughter didn't have to work so hard and could spend more of her time playing and enjoying herself, like other children.

When they got to the car park, the boys helped unload the shopping into the car and then watched as a rather clever lift arrangement hoisted Sophie's mother, still in her wheelchair, into the driver's seat.

'You were right,' Callum said as they made their way back to the cafe.

'About what?'

'When you said it wouldn't be a good idea to spray Sophie with the fire extinguisher.' Callum gave an embarrassed grin.

'Ah,' said Alex.

'Because if you *had* done it, and then we'd realized she was coming to ask us to help with her mum and . . . well, we'd have felt terrible, wouldn't we? That would have been a *real* mistake!'

'Yes,' Alex agreed. 'Yes, it would.'

It was always much harder for Callum to get his head round the idea of Ctrl-Z than for Alex. The problem for Callum was that, although Alex had explained to him several times how the laptop could take you back in time to before you had done anything bad, Callum had no memory of any occasion when this had actually happened. He had never actually *seen* Alex drive his mother's car out of the garage or upset a thousand cans of beans at the supermarket – or at least he had no memory of seeing these things.

Alex had been using Ctrl-Z every day since the

parcel from Godfather John first arrived, and could remember everything – but Callum did not. When Alex carried the china out to the garden and began throwing it at the rockery, Callum couldn't *know* – in the way that Alex did – that it was going to be all right. He had to trust each time that Ctrl-Z really did exist and that his friend had not gone quietly mad.

But although it was difficult, Callum *did* believe in Ctrl-Z. He believed in it partly because Alex was not the sort of person who made things up, and partly because his friend had shown an uncanny ability to know what was about to happen – but mostly because he had stopped having accidents.

In the week since the morning of Lilly's party, when Alex had come round with his laptop, Callum had not had a single accident. Not one. Alex told him that he had – that in the last two days alone, he had had accidents with a stapler, an electric carving knife and a nasty incident when his hair got caught in a light socket – but Callum didn't remember any of them. As far as he was concerned, he had had no accidents at all and, for someone who'd been coping with them for most of his life, this was truly remarkable.

Ctrl-Z might not be an easy explanation to believe, but it was the only one Callum had and he *did* believe it now, as completely as Alex did.

And he knew that, whenever he did have an accident, the first thing to do was tell Alex, so that he could press the keys on his computer.

And it was this, strangely enough, that nearly brought the whole glorious adventure to an end.

CHAPTER SEVEN

It was a Saturday morning, two weeks after Alex had got Ctrl-Z from Godfather John, and he had been sent down to the little row of shops in the Causeway to get some milk. It was a fifteen-minute walk, but he didn't mind. The sun was shining and his mother had told him he could buy himself an ice cream while he was there.

In the shop, he collected the milk and the ice cream and took them over to the counter.

'Two pounds twenty-seven, please,' said Mrs Bellini, and she took the ten-pound note Alex offered her and passed back his change.

Outside the shop, Alex sat himself on a bench that looked out over the river and was contentedly eating his ice cream when the river and the road in

71

front of him disappeared and he found himself back in the shop, standing in front of Mrs Bellini.

'Two pounds twenty-seven, please,' she said.

'What?' Alex stared at her.

'Two pounds twenty-seven,' Mrs Bellini repeated patiently. 'For the milk and the ice cream.'

By the third time this happened, Alex had worked out what was going on, or thought he had. Looking at his watch, he could see it was almost exactly ten o'clock when Mrs Bellini asked for the money, and four minutes past the hour when time stopped and he went back to being in the shop. Someone, somewhere, must have gone into his bedroom at home at four minutes past ten and pressed Ctrl-Z.

It could only be Callum, he thought. No one but Callum would have turned on the computer, gone to the page that set the time, changed it to ten o'clock and then pressed Ctrl-Z. Goodness only knew why he was doing it, but that wasn't important at the moment. What Alex needed to do was get back to the house before Callum pressed the button, otherwise he was going to be stuck repeating the same few minutes of time over and over again.

Walking from the shop back to the house, Alex knew, took between ten and fifteen minutes depending on how fast you walked. If he ran as fast as he could, he ought to be able to get back in time.

He was wrong.

The first time he tried it he was only three quarters of the way home before he found himself back in the shop with Mrs Bellini asking for her two pounds twenty-seven. He tried it three times more, each time running flat out as fast as he could, but it made no difference. Even when he abandoned the milk and ice cream and started running before Mrs Bellini had a chance to tell him how much he should pay, even when he took the short cut down the back of Exeter Street, he still couldn't get to Oakwood Close before four minutes past ten.

'Two pounds twenty-seven, please,' said Mrs Bellini.

As he handed over his ten-pound note for the ninth time, Alex tried to think. He *had* to get home in time to stop Callum pressing Ctrl-Z, and if he couldn't run there fast enough, then . . . He looked thoughtfully through the shop doorway to where two girls were talking on the pavement outside. One of them, he noticed, had a bicycle.

It took several tries before Alex could get hold of the bike. He began by asking the girl if he could borrow it, but she said no. Next, he tried offering her money, but she still said no, so then he tried snatching it from her, but that didn't work either. The little girl was only eight years old, but she clung ferociously to her bicycle, her fingers wrapped tightly round the handlebars. With her friend screaming for help, Alex could never quite wrench the bike free before the girl's mother came out of the shop, grabbed him by the collar and shouted for someone to call the police.

In the end, he found a simpler way. When Mrs Bellini asked for her two pounds twenty-seven, he left the ten-pound note on the counter, walked out of the shop, went straight over to the girls and told them their mother wanted them inside to choose which sweets they wanted. The girl left her bike leaning up against a pillar box and, as she walked towards the shop, Alex grabbed it and pedalled off.

It wasn't an easy bike to ride – it was smaller than he was used to and had no gears – but it was still faster than running. Pedalling as fast as he could, and with the cries of the girls and their mother fading behind him as he rode, Alex dashed along the Causeway, turned left into Roseby Crescent, raced up the hill along Derby Road and . . . and he very nearly made it.

Turning into the close he could actually see Callum running past the side of the house towards the back door and his mother standing by her car in the driveway. He opened his mouth to shout to Callum not to go indoors when –

'Two pounds twenty-seven, please,' said Mrs Bellini.

He tried the bicycle trick twice more, but it made no difference and, handing over the money for the seventeenth time, it dawned on Alex that he was in serious trouble. Unless he could get home before Callum pressed Ctrl-Z, he was going to be stuck in the same four minutes of time . . . forever.

In desperation, he considered stealing a car and was actually working out how he could snatch the keys from the woman behind him in the queue at the shop when he realized he didn't have to steal a car at all. There was a much simpler solution to his problem and he couldn't understand why he hadn't thought of it before.

'Two pounds twenty-seven, please,' said Mrs Bellini.

Alex gave her the ten-pound note. 'Could I use your phone to call my mum?' he said. 'I can pay you for it. Only it's quite urgent.'

'Yes, of course, dear.' Mrs Bellini pushed the phone across the counter towards him. 'And don't worry about paying.'

'Thanks.' Alex was already tapping in the number.

The phone rang for some time and he remembered his mother had been outside doing something to her car.

'Hello?' His mother's voice finally answered the call.

'Mum? It's me.'

'Alex? What are you –'

'Just listen, will you, Mum? You mustn't let Callum into the house, all right? When he calls round, don't let him in and don't let him up to my bedroom. It's really important, OK?'

'OK,' said his mother. 'Look, are you all right? Why are you –'

'I'm fine. I'll explain when I get home,' said Alex, and hung up.

When Alex turned into the drive of number 17 Oakwood Close, his mother swung herself out from under the back axle of the TR4.

'You were right,' she said. 'Callum came round just after you phoned. He told me to tell you he'd had an accident. Just after ten o'clock. He said it was very important you knew the time.'

'What sort of accident?' asked Alex.

'As far as I could tell, he was playing darts and one of them landed in his father's foot,' said Mrs Howard. 'But I couldn't get the details because his father was shouting for him to come home.

He was hopping mad. Literally.' Mrs Howard looked up at Alex. 'So how did you know?'

'What?'

'The phone call,' said Mrs Howard. 'The "Don't let Callum into the house" thing. How did you know he was coming and why did I have to keep him out of your room?'

'Oh, that,' said Alex. 'I . . . I'll just put this milk in the fridge, shall I? Then I'll explain it to you.'

Indoors, he left the milk on the table and went upstairs to his computer.

It was five minutes to ten and Callum was playing darts. The hook that normally held his dartboard to the wall had come out, so he propped it up on the window sill instead and he was about to start throwing when Alex appeared.

'Hi,' said Callum. 'Want a game?'

'No, thank you,' said Alex. 'One of the things I came to tell you is that playing darts by an open window, especially when your dad is standing underneath, is definitely a mistake. But sit down, will you? And listen.'

'OK.' Callum sat down on the bed. 'Has something happened?'

'I want you to imagine,' said Alex, ignoring the question, 'that you're up here throwing darts at that board and one of the darts misses the board, goes out of the window, and lands in your dad's foot, down in the garden. What would you do if that happened?'

'Well, I'd . . .' Callum hesitated. 'We're not talking about something I already did, are we?'

'Yes,' said Alex, 'but stay with the question for a minute; what would you do?'

'Well, I'd phone you and –'

'There isn't time to phone,' said Alex. 'Your dad's screaming that he's going to bury you in concrete . . .'

'Oh . . . well . . . I'd go round to your house . . .'

'Right,' said Alex. 'You come round to my house, but I'm not in. I've gone down to the shops. So what do you do then?'

There was something in the intensity of Alex's gaze that made Callum feel distinctly uncomfortable.

'Well . . .' he said, 'I suppose I'd go upstairs and try using Ctrl-Z on your computer to –'

'That is exactly what you did!' said Alex. 'And you must *never* do it again!'

'OK.' Callum looked puzzled. 'Why?'

'Because you hadn't told me, had you? So you went back in time, but you didn't know you had! You were just back here in your room playing darts and one of them went out of the window and hurt your dad, so you ran up to my house, set the computer, pressed Ctrl-Z so you were back here in your room playing darts and one of them went out of the window and hurt your dad, so you ran up to my house and set the computer . . . !'

'Oh . . .' You could almost see the cogs turning in Callum's brain as he worked out what this meant. 'What . . . what happened?'

Alex told him the whole story. About finding himself at the shop with Mrs Bellini every four minutes, about trying to get home to reset Ctrl-Z, about taking the bicycle and nearly stealing a car and, finally, about the phone call.

'You must never,' said Alex, '*never* press Ctrl-Z without telling me first, so that I can tell you what you need not to do. OK?'

'Right,' said Callum. 'OK.'

That night, Alex wrote an email to his godfather, telling him what had happened. It had been a bit of a shock to realize that his laptop could be quite so dangerous and he wondered if there were any other risks in using it. If there were, he wrote, it would be good to be warned about them so that in future he could try to avoid them.

The reply, when it arrived, was not as helpful as he'd hoped.

Dear Alex, it said,

*It sounds like you've been making some import-
ant mistakes. Well done! And in answer to your
question: yes, there are plenty more dangers in
using Ctrl-Z. My advice is to be very careful!*

*And I thought I'd mention there's a chance I
may be travelling to Europe some time in the next
couple of months – so perhaps I'll have a chance
to call in and hear from you directly how you're
getting on.*

In the meantime, take care!
Your loving godfather
John Presley

'*Plenty more dangers . . .*' Alex read the phrase
again.

It wasn't exactly encouraging.

CHAPTER EIGHT

Having Ctrl-Z might cause Alex the occasional scare, but nothing would have persuaded him to give it up. It was by far the most exciting present he had ever received and being able to walk out of school in the middle of the morning or suddenly decide to borrow his mother's car meant Ctrl-Z was worth any of the risks involved.

And in the days that followed, Alex discovered his laptop was useful in more ways than he had expected. For a start, it meant that life became almost totally pain-free. If he accidentally cut himself on a bit of broken glass, or grazed his elbow when he fell off his bike, or did something as simple as stubbing his toe on a chair leg, with Ctrl-Z all Alex had to do was go back to before it had happened and the pain was gone as completely as if it had never been there – which of course it hadn't.

With Ctrl-Z, if you were watching a DVD and you were only halfway through it when Dad said it was time for bed, you could go back an hour and watch the second half. If there was a meal you particularly enjoyed you could go back and eat it all over again – and eat it as many times as you liked without getting full because each time you went back, you went back to being as hungry as you were the first time. And if you bought something in a shop, like a computer game, you could have all the fun of playing with it for a few hours and then, if you didn't want to keep it, go back to before you'd bought it and buy something else.

But there was one other thing Ctrl-Z could do that was, in its own way, better than any of those. It was better than never getting hurt, better than undoing Callum's accidents, and even better than the excitement of breaking all the windows in a greenhouse. With Ctrl-Z, Alex found, it was possible to make sure that everything went *right*.

Everything.

When Callum rang up to point out that they had missed their favourite TV programme, Alex could go back to when it had started and set the recorder. When Mum left her handbag in a shop, with all her money and her credit cards in it and was convinced it had been stolen, Alex simply rewound time to when it happened and reminded her to pick it up from the counter. And when Dad got back late to the car park after a trip to the swimming pool and found he had a parking fine, Alex went back to make sure he bought a ticket for the time he would need. And had another swim.

Everything went so much more smoothly with Ctrl-Z. With his laptop, Alex could iron out all the little irritations and annoyances that might disturb the even flow of life before they ever happened. In school or at home, when the day hit a wrinkle, it was no problem. You just went back and made the wrinkle disappear. Dad taking a wrong turning in the car, someone spilling tea on the carpet, Mum hitting her thumb with a hammer – whatever it was, you simply went back and made sure it didn't happen. All at the click of a key on the computer.

And for Alex, the wrinkle that he was particularly glad to smooth out – the one that had, until recently, made him the most uncomfortable – was the way his parents kept having arguments.

The simplest way to stop his parents arguing, and the one Alex used most often, was to find out the cause and put it right before it happened. If he found them arguing, for instance, about who should have emptied the bin, he would go back and empty it himself so they had nothing to argue about.

A lot of the time this was what worked best, but it wasn't always that easy. Sometimes the arguments were about things that Alex couldn't change, even with Ctrl-Z. His parents had a huge argument, for instance, the day his mother's car broke down on the way to a job interview, and there wasn't much Alex could do about that. Even with Ctrl-Z he couldn't fix a faulty distributor.

Mrs Howard had been working for some years to pass the exams she needed to get a job, like her husband, as an accountant. The plan was that, after she had got some experience working with a local firm, the two of them would set up an accountancy partnership together. It was a dream they had had almost from the time they had got married, but at the moment it seemed to have stalled.

There were not that many opportunities to work locally as an accountant and when they did come up, there always seemed to be a reason why Mrs Howard didn't get the job. When she didn't even get to the interview because her car broke down, they had one of their worst arguments ever, with Mr Howard saying Mrs Howard should have allowed more time and Mrs Howard throwing half a pound of butter at Mr Howard's head.

On occasions like this, although there was nothing Alex could do to stop the cause of the argument, he found he could at least defuse the situation. His parents tended not to argue if he was in the same room, and if he went back and made sure he *was* in the same room when the row started, it usually meant the argument never properly got off the ground.

It wasn't perfect, but it was a big improvement and sometimes he could do even better than that.

The worst argument his parents had, and the one Alex was particularly proud of sorting out, was the one they had on his mother's birthday. It was the Wednesday of half-term and his father had taken Alex into town to collect the birthday present he had bought for his wife.

Standing in the middle of a brightly lit car showroom, he patted the bonnet of a brand-new silver Toyota and grinned at Alex.

'There!' he said. 'You think she'll like it?'

'You're buying Mum a *car* for her birthday?' said Alex. 'I thought she said she wanted an engine hoist?'

'I know!' His father's smile grew even broader. 'This is going to be a real surprise! I chose it last week and all I have to do now is pay for it. With this.' He held out a banker's draft. 'It means she won't break down on the way to important interviews any more. And she won't have to spend all her spare time repairing that old Triumph, either. She'll be able to concentrate on getting the sort of job she deserves!'

When Mrs Howard got home at four o'clock that day, swinging her bicycle on to the driveway, Alex and his father were waiting for her, standing either side of the new car. Mr Howard had got a huge piece of pink ribbon and tied it round the middle into a big bow at the top, so that it looked like a real present.

Mrs Howard got off her bike and looked at it.

'What's this?' she said.

'It's for you,' said Mr Howard proudly.

'Happy birthday!' said Alex.

Mrs Howard stepped forward to examine the Toyota.

'I thought I told you I wanted an engine hoist,' she said.

'I know,' said Mr Howard happily, 'but I got you this.'

'I've already got a car,' said Mrs Howard.

'But this one,' said Mr Howard, 'is completely reliable! You can go to interviews, drive it to work – it'll never break down!'

'And what do I do with that?' Mrs Howard pointed to the Triumph in the garage.

'Well . . . you can sell it!'

'Sell it.' Mrs Howard looked at her husband. 'Of course. After I've spent two years doing it up, what else would I *want* to do but sell it?'

'Look,' said Mr Howard, beginning to sound rather cross, 'I think the least you can do after I've spent all that money is –'

'Yes, that's the other thing,' interrupted Mrs Howard. 'You spent all that money without talking to me about it first?'

Mr Howard stared at her. 'I can't believe this! You are *angry* with me for buying you a car?'

'Yes, I am,' said Mrs Howard. 'Very angry.'

'Oh, for goodness' sake!' Mr Howard was beginning to sound quite angry himself. 'We've been working for twelve years so that you can do something a bit more useful with your life than be a garage receptionist, and I thought at least you'd like –'

'No, you didn't!' said Mrs Howard. 'You didn't think what I might like at all. All you did was decide what *you* wanted, and then went ahead and did it!'

After that things followed a familiar pattern. The arguing got worse, the things that were said got more hurtful and the voices got louder and louder until they were both shouting so much that neither of them noticed Alex as he quietly walked back into the house and up to his room.

'There!' said his father, patting the bonnet of a silver Toyota. 'What do you think?'

'I think it's fantastic,' said Alex, 'but if you're getting it for Mum's birthday, I can tell you she won't like it.'

'What?' His father looked rather startled. 'What do you mean? How can she not like it? It's brand new. It won't break down on the way to interviews. It's –'

'She's already got a car,' said Alex. 'The Triumph.'

'Well, she can sell that!'

'She's been working on it for two years!' said Alex. 'Would you want to sell something you'd been working on for two years and only just finished?'

Mr Howard opened his mouth to speak, then closed it again.

'You need to trust me on this one, Dad,' said Alex firmly. 'Don't buy the car. Not till you've talked to Mum about it. It'd be a mistake. I know it would.'

There was something in the way his son spoke that made Mr Howard hesitate. Things had not been working out too well with Lois recently and he had been hoping that the present would improve things. But if Alex was right . . .

'Why don't you call her?' said Alex. 'Just to check it's what she'd really want.'

'If I call her,' said his father, 'it won't be a surprise.'

'If it *is* a surprise,' said Alex, 'it'll be a disaster. Honestly.'

Mr Howard said nothing for several seconds, then slowly took out his mobile and dialled his wife's number. The conversation he had was short, but left him in no doubt what he should do.

'Right.' He turned to Alex. 'Let's go and buy that engine hoist.'

Mrs Howard was delighted with her birthday present. It would mean, she pointed out, that she could get at the driveshaft housing without all the trouble of taking her car down to the garage. She gave her husband a huge hug and an embarrassingly soppy kiss, then sat down and opened her cards and her other presents. Later, she ate the supper Dad had cooked, and the cake he had bought and said at the end that it had been one of the nicest birthdays she could remember.

Mr Howard was pleased, you could see that, but Alex couldn't help noticing that his father was quieter than usual and, occasionally through the evening, he would look at his wife with a puzzled expression, as if there was something about her that he simply didn't understand. He had wanted to buy her a really expensive present, something that would be useful as well as smart, something she really needed . . . and for some reason it was not what she wanted.

He wondered, sometimes, if he understood her at all.

Alex was puzzled as well. The two birthdays could not have been more different, he thought. If you'd seen how furious his mother was the first time round and how his parents had shouted and yelled, you'd have thought they hated each other and were heading for a divorce. And yet, when the same two people came together with a different birthday present, they had both been happy and full of smiles and everything had been just like the old days. Why, he wondered, should what you got for your birthday make so much difference?

Not that he was objecting. With Ctrl-Z, he had managed to make things turn out right, and that was the best thing about having his laptop, really.

That you could make *everything* turn out right.

CHAPTER NINE

Alex was not the only one who appreciated the effects of Ctrl-Z. Life for his friend Callum had not simply got better, it had been transformed.

Callum had been accident-prone for almost as long as he could remember and however hard he tried, he had never found a way to stop it. A psychologist had once suggested that the accidents happened because he was always worrying that they might, but as Callum pointed out, he only worried because the accidents *did* happen – and it was very hard not to worry if you walked through life knowing that disaster was always only a footstep away.

In the last few weeks, however, all that had changed. Since Alex had been given the laptop,

Callum had not had any accidents at all. None, at least, that he could remember, and for the first time in years the anxiety that had once been his constant companion had eased. He no longer walked everywhere with the worry at the back of his mind that something bad was about to happen because . . . well, because nothing bad *did* happen any more. And, apparently, if it ever did all he had to do was tell Alex and let him press a couple of keys on his computer.

The relief was almost indescribable. The tight ball of tension that Callum normally felt in the pit of his stomach had begun to unwind. The worry slipped away, and it was as if a great weight had been lifted from his shoulders. There was a relaxed ease in the way Callum walked these days, a calm in the face of any situation that he had never shown before and – and this was the really odd thing – he *didn't* have as many accidents now. In fact, fewer and fewer all the time.

When Alex had first got his laptop, he could expect to rescue his friend from some disaster at least once or twice a day but, as the weeks passed, that number had steadily dwindled. Maybe the psychologist had been right and, now that he was less anxious, Callum was no longer drawing the accidents into his life. Alex didn't know, but he did know that his friend had changed.

Mr and Mrs Bannister had noticed it as well.

'I hope you know how grateful we are,' Callum's mother told Alex one day as they were sitting out in the garden. She pointed to Callum standing at the barbecue in an apron, calmly cooking sausages. 'Look at him!' she said proudly. 'He's in charge of an open fire and we're not worried at all! It's like he's a different boy!' She beamed down at Alex. 'And we all know why, don't we!'

'Do we?' said Alex a little nervously. He had explained to Callum the importance of not saying anything to his parents about Ctrl-Z.

'It's you, isn't it!' Mrs Bannister placed an affectionate hand on his shoulder. 'Callum's told us how you've been helping him. Talking to him. Teaching him how to stay out of trouble.'

'Oh, that . . .' said Alex.

'And whatever you've said to him, it's certainly worked.' Mr Bannister had come over to join them. 'We can't believe how much better he's been the last few weeks. It's a miracle.'

'Oh good,' said Alex.

'And because of that,' said Mrs Bannister, 'we were wondering if perhaps you'd be able to come on holiday with us this summer. Only it makes such a difference when you're around, and we thought –'

'We thought it'd be safer for all of us,' Mr

Bannister took over, 'if you came too. We're renting a villa in France. With a swimming pool. If you'd like, I'll have a word with your parents.'

And Alex said he thought a villa in France with a swimming pool would be . . . very nice. Thank you!

The one thing Alex hadn't been able to do with his computer was use it to make money. Godfather John had said that, if he thought about it, he would find there were at least twenty-seven ways to make himself rich with Ctrl-Z – and Alex had thought about it, but without coming up with *one* idea, let alone twenty-seven. Not that it bothered him, really. At the moment, he was having too much fun.

One day he painted the sitting-room sofa blue (to see what it looked like); on another he experimented with putting half a dozen eggs in the microwave to see if they'd explode (they did); and on another he nailed a set of planks to the staircase so that he could use it as a ski run. In fact he did all the things that a boy his age might want to do if he knew they wouldn't get into trouble for doing them.

So, when he found a box of fireworks in the back of the cupboard in the dining room that his father used as an office, there was never any doubt about what Alex would do with them. He only had to look at the box to see they were begging to be set off.

It was a Saturday, and Alex had just set the time on his computer and collected the box from its hiding place when Callum appeared at the front door.

'We're going down to the park,' he said, gesturing to the pavement where he had left Lilly in her wheelchair, holding Mojo the dog on a lead. 'Lilly wants to feed the ducks and says can you come too.'

'I've got a better idea,' said Alex, and showed his friend the fireworks. 'Dad's gone to a conference and Mum's not back for an hour, so we can let them off now. In the garden!'

'If you let them off,' said Callum, 'won't your dad notice they've gone?'

'They won't *be* gone, will they!' Alex reminded him. 'We fire them off, I press Ctrl-Z and they're back in the box in the cupboard!'

'Yes . . .' said Callum doubtfully. It was the same every time Alex suggested something like this. He would hesitate and wonder if it was safe. And fireworks definitely *weren't* safe. Everyone knew that.

'I'm not sure if Lilly –'

'Lilly'll be fine!' Alex interrupted him confidently. 'She'll like the fireworks and afterwards she won't remember, will she? Neither of you will.'

Callum wheeled Lilly round to the back of the house, Alex locked Mojo in the kitchen and the two boys picked up a couple of fireworks out of the box and took them down the garden. The results were, to be honest, a little disappointing. Fireworks look their best at night when the coloured flames shine out against the dark, but in the middle of a summer's afternoon it was difficult to see anything at all. The fireworks made quite a bit of noise as well, and Alex knew it wouldn't be long before someone like Mr Kowalski came round to complain.

'You should try this one next,' Lilly told them. She had taken the largest firework from the bottom of the box and passed it to Callum. It was called The Mortar and was about the size of a large tin can on a stick. The instructions said to place the stick firmly in the ground, light the fuse and stand well back, so Alex took it down to the bottom of the garden, pushed the stick firmly into the soil and then Callum lit the blue touchpaper and they both ran back to stand by Lilly on the patio.

Nothing happened. They waited for nearly a minute, but still nothing happened.

'It must have gone out,' said Alex, and he was heading down the garden with the matches to light it again when Callum stopped him.

'You're not supposed to go back to a firework once you've lit it,' he said. 'You have to wait.'

'How long for?' asked Alex.

'I think at least an hour,' said Callum. 'You don't want to have it explode in your face, do you?'

'I need a drink,' said Lilly, and Alex opened the back door so that she could wheel herself into the kitchen.

He had forgotten about Mojo. Locked inside the house, the dog knew that he had been missing out on all the excitement and now that he was out in the open, he was determined to make the most of it.

Mojo's favourite games usually involved either a ball or a stick, and racing down the garden he found a stick in the earth at the far edge of the lawn. Perfect! He grabbed it in his teeth and did what all sensible dogs do with a stick – he carried it back to his master.

Callum had been right when he told Alex that you should never go back to a firework once you had lit it. The blue touchpaper of The Mortar had been slightly damp, but it was still smouldering. Now, with the air blowing past it as Mojo raced down the garden it suddenly ignited and a moment later balls of phosphorous began bursting from the can at the end of the stick.

If The Mortar had been stuck in the ground,

the balls of fire would have shot up into the air, but because Mojo was holding the stick in his teeth, they shot out sideways. The first of them travelled across the ground at about knee height, straight towards Callum.

Callum squeaked in panic and stepped to one side, but there were already others following. In a series of dazzling colours, they shot out from the firework to splatter all over the garden. One of them went into the fence, another flew *over* the fence to land on top of Mr Kowalski's shed, and two more flew towards the house. The first of them bounced harmlessly off the brick, but the other went straight through the open back door into the kitchen.

There was a faint *whoompf* as the burning ball landed in a bowl of paraffin that Mrs Howard had been using to soak the grease from a section of engine mounting, and ignited. The bowl was actually an old ice-cream tub, and two seconds later, one side of the tub melted in the heat of the flames and the paraffin, still alight, poured out on to the floor.

The pool of fire spread rapidly from the back door to the door that led into the hall and then over towards the sink, where Lilly was in her wheelchair, getting herself a drink. The flickering blue flames meant she was trapped, Alex realized.

The burning paraffin cut her off from both the back door and the door to the hallway and there was no way out. She looked across at Alex. She didn't say anything, but her eyes were wide and frightened.

By now the newspaper Mrs Howard had placed under the tub of paraffin to catch any drips was alight as well and burning fiercely in the doorway. There was a *pop* as something in one of the kitchen cupboards exploded in the heat and there were more flames licking up the varnish on the door to the hall.

What Alex needed to do was press Ctrl-Z, but his computer was in the dining room. He had left it there when he collected the fireworks – ready and set with the time before he started so that all he had to do was walk in and press Ctrl-Z – and now he couldn't get to it without walking through burning paraffin. There was no other way into the house. The front door was locked and there were no windows open. The only way to the dining room was through the knee-high flames and he didn't think he could do it. He didn't even have shoes on . . .

Callum appeared, white-faced, beside Alex. The boys watched, frozen, as the flames moved across the floor until they were lapping at the wheels of Lilly's chair. She screamed.

'Hang on!' said Callum. 'I'm coming . . .'

Alex pulled him back. It might sound callous, but he knew the important thing was not to rescue Lilly, but to get through to his computer. 'I'll go,' he said, and was about to step into the fire when a hand descended on his shoulder and pulled him back.

It was Mr Kowalski, old Mr Kowalski with his unshaven chin and his cardigan with the holes in the elbows, and he was pushing both boys away from the door.

'Stay back,' he said gruffly. 'Both of you!' And then he was walking into the kitchen, taking no more notice of the flames around his feet than if he were wading through a patch of long grass, and he was scooping Lilly up and out of the wheelchair and carrying her in his arms with long, careful strides back through the door and out into the garden and safety.

'Everything OK,' he was murmuring to her, his voice nothing like the rough tones he normally used. 'Everything all right. No worry . . .' One hand was stroking her hair and he looked carefully along her body. 'You hurt?'

Lilly shook her head.

'Mr Kowalski,' said Callum, 'your trousers are on fire.'

Some of the burning paraffin had splashed up

on to Mr Kowalski's clothes and little flames were spotted over his shoes and the bottom half of his trousers. Mr Kowalski ignored them as he turned to Alex.

'Go next door. Quick,' he said. 'Phone fire brigade.' Then he placed Lilly carefully on the grass before beating out the flames on his trousers with his hands.

Alex ran along the side of the house, his heart pounding, and when he got to the front, did what he realized he ought to have done when the fire first started. He picked up a large rock from the front garden and threw it as hard as he could towards the sitting-room window. The glass shattered, Alex reached in through the hole to undo the catch, opened the window and climbed inside.

In the hallway he could see that some of the paraffin had leaked under the kitchen door and was burning on the hall carpet, but he ignored it and ran into the dining room. The computer was sitting on the table and all he had to do was reach out to it . . .

. . . and press Ctrl-Z.

'We're going down to the park,' said Callum, gesturing to the pavement where he had left Lilly in her wheelchair, holding Mojo the dog on a lead.

'Lilly wants to feed the ducks and says can you come too.'

'Oh,' said Alex. 'Right . . .' It was taking him a moment to catch his breath.

'What have you got in there?' Callum pointed to the box of fireworks Alex was holding.

'Nothing,' said Alex. 'I was just . . . tidying up.'

'Are you coming or not?' Lilly called from the pavement.

'Yes,' said Alex. 'Yes, I'm coming. Definitely.'

It was one of those times, he thought, when feeding the ducks was about as much excitement as he wanted.

CHAPTER TEN

The incident with the fireworks was a sharp reminder to Alex that if he was going to do anything dangerous, he needed to make sure that either he or Callum was standing very close to the Ctrl-Z button, preferably with a finger poised, ready to push down the moment anything went wrong.

As it happened, nobody had been hurt, but the more he thought about it the more Alex realized he had been very lucky. If Mr Kowalski had not appeared when he did, if the flames had moved a little closer to Lilly, if he had tried to run across the kitchen and failed . . . it could all have ended very differently.

In the days that followed, Alex found he couldn't stop thinking about it. At odd times during the day pictures of what had happened would flash into his mind and he would find himself going through the whole business again in his head. Try as he might, he couldn't make the pictures go away and the image that came up most determinedly was of Mr Kowalski. Mr Kowalski pulling him back from the door . . . Mr Kowalski walking through the flames to scoop Lilly up into his arms . . . Mr Kowalski with his trousers on fire calmly putting her down on the grass before beating out the flames with his hands . . .

Alex had always thought of his neighbour as a grumpy old man who only spoke if he wanted to complain, but he knew now that he had been mistaken. Mr Kowalski might be old and grumpy and shoot at dogs in his garden with an air pistol, but he was more than that. Mr Kowalski was . . . a hero. On the day the kitchen caught fire he had shown the sort of courage you read about in stories and had walked into the flames to save Lilly's life at the risk of his own. He probably deserved a medal.

The trouble was that nobody *knew* Mr Kowalski was a hero. Not even Mr Kowalski. Alex wanted to tell him how grateful he was for what he had done and how much he admired him, but he couldn't do anything like that because Mr Kowalski wouldn't know what he was talking about. How could you say thank you to someone for something they didn't know they'd done?

It was Sophie Reynolds who gave him the answer when she came into school two days later and presented him with a cake that she said she had baked herself.

Sophie had behaved differently to both Alex and Callum ever since that day at the shopping mall. These days, she smiled and said hello when she saw them in the morning, she lent Callum a pen when his own had run out of ink, and she sorted out Alex when he had a problem with his maths. The boys didn't mind this, but baking him a cake was, Alex thought, going too far and it was quite a relief when Sophie said it was not for him.

'It's for your mum,' she said. 'For what she did on Friday.'

The previous Friday, driving into town, Alex had seen Sophie and her mother with their car stopped by the side of the road. The bonnet was up and Mrs Reynolds was in her wheelchair, peering anxiously at the engine.

They had stopped to see if they could help. In the close, most people came to Mrs Howard if anything went wrong with their cars; even if she couldn't fix it herself, she could almost always tell you what the fault was and what you should do about it. In this case, Alex's mother had found a loose connection to the battery and dealt with it in a matter of seconds.

'They should have spotted that at the service,' she told Sophie's mother as she closed the bonnet. 'You should come to us next time. It wouldn't happen where I work.'

The cake Sophie had made was a large Victoria sponge, lavishly filled with strawberries and cream.

'Mum likes strawberries,' said Alex. 'It looks good. Thanks.' And it was the cake looking so good that gave him his idea.

He couldn't say thank you to Mr Kowalski in words because words were no use when you wanted to thank someone for something that had, technically, never happened . . .

. . . But you could bake them a cake.

Alex made the cake after school the next day. Sophie gave him the recipe and his mother found him the ingredients, though he insisted on doing all the work himself. He wanted it to be *his* cake, and the result wasn't bad. He only had to use Ctrl-Z twice while he was making it – once when he put in the wrong number of eggs and a second time when he forgot to take it out of the oven – but the result was quite tasty. He and Callum tried a slice themselves when it was finished, and then

Alex used Ctrl-Z to go back to before they had eaten it, and took the cake round to number 16.

It was some time before Mr Kowalski came shuffling along the hall in his slippers to answer the bell, and when he opened the door he frowned down at Alex.

'What you want?' he demanded.

'I came to give you this,' said Alex, holding out the cake.

'This?' Mr Kowalski looked at the cake and then at Alex. 'Is some sort of joke?'

'It's not a joke,' said Alex patiently. 'It's a cake.'

'Why?' asked Mr Kowalski suspiciously. 'Why you give me cake?'

'Well, I thought you'd like it,' said Alex, 'and I . . .' He took a deep breath. 'I wanted to say sorry. For all the things coming over the fence into your garden. It must have been very annoying, and I wanted to apologize for any inconvenience it may have caused.'

Mr Kowalski stared at him for a moment, then took the cake and without a word closed the door. Alex didn't mind. His neighbour could be as grumpy as he liked, it wasn't going to make any difference to how Alex felt about him.

And, grumpy or not, Mr Kowalski had at least taken the cake.

*

Two hours later Alex was lying upstairs on his bed, listening to his parents downstairs in the kitchen having an argument. They were arguing, as far as he could tell, about whether his mother should apply for a job that was advertised in the paper. His mother thought the job was too far away and didn't want to spend half her day travelling, and Mr Howard was telling her that when you started out you needed to go for any job you could get.

They weren't actually shouting at each other yet, but Alex suspected it was only a matter of time and was wondering whether it was better to go down now or to wait. He was still trying to decide when the front doorbell rang.

Mr Howard answered it and found Mr Kowalski standing in the porch, though at first he hardly recognized him. Instead of the cardigan hc usually wore, with the holes in the elbows, he was dressed in a suit. It was clean, freshly pressed and there was a gold watch chain hanging across the waist-coat. Mr Kowalski looked clean and freshly pressed himself. He had shaved and he was wearing a hat, which he took off when Mr Howard opened the door.

'Apologies if I disturb, Mr Howard,' he said. 'Is possible I speak to your son?'

'Yes, of course,' said Mr Howard, and he called up the stairs. 'Alex? Down here, please!' He turned back to Mr Kowalski. 'Has he done something to annoy you? Because if he has –'

'No, no, he is no trouble.' Mr Kowalski looked slightly embarrassed. 'He give me cake.'

'Cake?' Mr Howard looked puzzled. 'What . . . you mean as a joke?'

'Was not a joke,' said Mr Kowalski. 'Was a cake. But I not polite. Very bad manners.' He looked up as Alex appeared on the stairs and smiled. 'So I come now to say thank you.' Still smiling, he clicked his heels and gave Alex a little bow. 'And to say that cake was . . . much appreciated.'

'Oh,' said Alex. 'Good.'

'And I bring you these.' Mr Kowalski produced a bag and, reaching inside, took out a cricket ball, three tennis balls, a frisbee and a football. 'I find them in my garden. They are yours, yes?'

'Yes! That's great!' They were all the things that Alex had lost over the fence during the last few months – all, that is, except the football, which seemed to be new. 'This one isn't mine,' he said, passing it back.

'No?' Mr Kowalski gave a little shrug. 'You keep it anyway, eh? Play football with your friends!'

'Right,' said Alex. 'Thanks very much.'

'Mr Kowalski!' Alex's mother had come out of the kitchen. 'How nice to see you. Would you like a drink?'

'Well . . .' Mr Kowalski hesitated. 'I not want to disturb . . .'

'Come on!' Mrs Howard took his arm and led him down the hallway. 'We haven't seen you for ages. We don't often get a chance to talk.'

Mr Kowalski stayed for a drink, then a second one and then stayed for supper. One way and another it was a surprisingly jolly evening. The four of them sat round the kitchen table and talked. They talked about Alex's cake, they talked about jobs and work, they talked about cars – and then somehow the conversation came round to Callum and his accidents. Mr Kowalski said that he had had a lot of accidents when he was growing up in Poland and then Mr Howard started talking about things he had done as a boy that were every bit as disastrous as anything Callum had done and Alex found it all very interesting. Best of all, while they were talking, nobody argued about anything.

It was after Mr Kowalski had gone and they were doing the dishes that Alex's mother remarked how strange it all was.

'How do you mean?' asked Mr Howard.

'Well,' she said, 'we've always thought Mr Kowalski didn't like people – he never lets anyone into his house, he hardly says good morning – and then he comes round here and talks like that for nearly three hours. Why?'

'Perhaps he's changed,' said Mr Howard. 'Like Callum.'

'And why does he hate animals and children so much?' Alex's mother went on. 'Why's he so desperate to keep them out of his garden?'

'A lot of people don't like animals and children.' Mr Howard smiled at Alex. 'Perfectly understandable.'

'And what's with keeping his curtains drawn all the time?' said Mrs Howard, scrubbing at the last of the saucepans. 'And all the windows tightly closed. Can you imagine how hot it must get in there?'

'Perhaps he's hiding something,' said Mr Howard.

'Hiding something . . . ?' Mrs Howard frowned. 'Like what?'

'That,' said her husband, slowly shaking his head, 'is something we shall probably never know.'

And in that moment it occurred to Alex that something else you could do with Ctrl-Z, was solve a mystery like Mr Kowalski in a blink.

Chapter Eleven

'What we have to do,' Alex told Callum as they walked to school the next morning, 'is wait until he goes out, then I'll go into his house and take a look around and see what he's hiding.'

'How are you going to get in?' asked Callum. 'He'll have locked the door when he goes out, won't he?'

Alex had thought of that. He had considered throwing a brick through one of the windows and breaking in, but decided there was no need.

'He doesn't lock the door when he's just going out to the garden,' he said, 'and he's out there every day. At four o'clock he has his tea sitting on the bench and usually falls asleep. He'll be out there for at least half an hour.'

Callum thought the whole thing sounded very risky and said so.

'Oh, come on!' said Alex. 'I'm not asking you to come with me or anything! I just need you to keep watch. If you see him move back to the house, you press Ctrl-Z. That's all you have to do!'

Alex had thought of taking the laptop with him, but then remembered the time he had carried it into Mr Kowalski's garden and dropped it. It would be safer to leave it with Callum.

Callum still did not like the idea.

'If something goes wrong . . .' he said.

'It wouldn't matter if anything *did* go wrong, would it!' interrupted Alex. 'Because if it did, all you've got to do is press Ctrl-Z!'

Callum sighed. Since his accidents had stopped, life had been wonderfully calm and peaceful, and he felt a strong reluctance to do anything that might threaten that. On the other hand, it was very hard to say no to someone who had, only the day before, warned him that Lilly was about to abseil out of her window and suggested someone stop her before she fell and hurt herself.

Callum's sister was feeling a lot better these days and she had always been an adventurous girl. After the warning from Alex, Callum had gone to her bedroom and found her with one end of a length of rope tied round the bed and the other round her waist, about to climb out of the window. He had given her a long lecture on the need to behave sensibly when recovering from an illness.

Alex had known what was going to happen, of course, because it already had, and he had used Ctrl-Z to go back to before it happened so that Callum could stop it. When a friend did something like that for you, it was difficult to say no when he wanted a favour in return.

'All right,' he agreed.

'Great!' said Alex. 'We'll meet up in my room at about quarter to four.'

At exactly four o'clock, Mr Kowalski emerged from his back door with a mug of tea and a newspaper tucked under one arm. He strolled across his garden and settled himself comfortably on the bench.

Alex and Callum watched him from the window of Alex's bedroom.

'Right . . .' Alex pointed to the computer screen on his desk. 'The time's all set. You remember what you have to do?'

'I keep my eyes on Mr Kowalski,' said Callum. 'If I see him coming back to the house, I press Ctrl-Z.'

'And?'

'And if you haven't come out after ten minutes, I press the button anyway.'

'That's right,' said Alex. 'And don't look so worried. I keep telling you. Nothing can go wrong!'

As he made his way downstairs and out of the front door, Alex could hear his mother working on her beloved Triumph in the garage and he smiled cheerfully to himself as he jumped over the low wall between his house and Mr Kowalski's. A moment later he was at the back door of number 16, quietly pushing it open and stepping inside.

It was dark in Mr Kowalski's kitchen, but once Alex's eyes got used to the light that filtered through the curtains and blinds, he could see the room was surprisingly neat and tidy. It was clean, everything looked normal, and he made his way through to the hall.

It was even darker here, though he had no trouble finding his way around. All the houses in Oakwood Close were built with the same floor plan and he looked briefly into the dining room – in his own house, his father used it as an office – before making his way through to the sitting room.

It was so dark in this room that it was almost impossible to see anything, and there was an odd, musty smell in the air that Alex couldn't quite place. He wondered about turning on a light, but decided not to in case Mr Kowalski noticed it from the garden, and went to the front window to pull back one of the curtains instead. It didn't move. Feeling with his hands, he found it had been nailed to the window sill.

He should have brought a torch, he thought. Even as his eyes got used to the dark, he couldn't see anything beyond the vaguest shapes, and he was wondering if he should go back to the house and get one, when he froze. He had heard a noise. It was a faint sort of rustling sound that he thought at first he might have imagined, but no . . . there it was again.

There was someone else in the room, and they were moving – moving quietly, but definitely towards him.

It was time to leave and Alex took a step towards the door – or tried to, but his legs wouldn't move. They seemed to be glued to the floor and try as he might he could not move them so much as an inch. There was something holding them, something wrapped around the lower half of his legs. Reaching down, Alex could feel something warm and slightly rough to the touch under his fingers, and he knew immediately what it was.

It was a snake.

It had to be a very large snake. There were two coils of it round the bottom of his legs, each of them almost as thick as Alex's waist, and they were heavy. He could feel the weight of them against his feet, and when he tried to push them away it was like pushing a wall. Nothing moved, except that the coils tightened slightly, increasing the pressure against his legs. There were three coils now instead of two and they were moving, winding themselves slowly further up his body.

Well, Alex thought, at least he had solved the mystery. He knew why Mr Kowalski kept the doors locked and curtains drawn now. If you had a large snake in your house you would want to make sure that it didn't get out. And you wouldn't let people inside, either. He had a feeling there were laws about keeping large and dangerous pets and the snake curled round his legs was certainly large . . .

The three coils had become four now and were still moving. As they passed his waist, Alex opened his mouth and began calling for help. He shouted, shouted as loudly as he could – it didn't matter now if Mr Kowalski came. In fact, he *wanted* him to appear. But he didn't. Nobody came. The double glazing fitted to the windows of the houses in the close was highly effective soundproofing and nobody heard.

The coils were up to his chest now and drawing tighter. It was getting difficult to breathe. Alex tried to think. How long would it be before Callum realized he had not come out and pressed Ctrl-Z.

He had told him to wait ten minutes and he had a nasty feeling that by then it would be too late.

Did Ctrl-Z still work after you'd died, Alex wondered? Could it bring you back to life and take you back to before it had happened? He had once joked about the possibility with Callum, but this wasn't a joke at all . . .

The coils covered his body up to the top of his chest now. His arms were pinned against his sides and breathing was almost impossible. It was an effort to expand his chest to pull in even the smallest gasp of air and he had given up shouting for help. Did snakes try to swallow you while you were still alive, he wondered? He didn't fancy that. Probably better to have someone hit you on the back of the head with a piece of piping than . . .

It was getting difficult to think. There were little coloured lights in front of his eyes and then suddenly –

Suddenly there was a bright light and the sound of someone's voice. '*Boze mój e!!*'

'Alex?' Mr Kowalski's face had appeared, slightly blurred, swimming in the air in front of him. 'You don't move! You hear me? You keep still!'

A slightly unnecessary instruction, Alex thought. There hadn't been much chance of moving for some time.

'Oh, you are bad boy! You are *very* bad boy!' Mr

Kowalski was saying, and Alex was trying to apologize when he realized the old man was talking to the snake. He had grabbed one end of it, the tail, and was unwinding the coils as he spoke. A bit later, the pressure on Alex's chest began to ease. He could breathe again and he sank to the floor. Slumping on the carpet, his back resting against the wall, he could actually see the snake for the first time.

It was truly enormous. Well over ten metres in length, its coils seemed to cover most of the floor. Mr Kowalski had a section of it slung over his shoulder and was hauling it across the room, pushing it into a huge wooden chest that ran along one wall. As he put one part of the snake in the chest, another would start to slide out and Mr Kowalski would determinedly grab it and push it back in, talking to it all the time as if it were a naughty child.

Finally, the last section of the snake had been stuffed into the box and Mr Kowalski closed the lid and snapped a bolt to keep it in place. He came back to Alex, knelt down and stared anxiously into his eyes.

'How are you, Alex? You all right?'

'I-I think so.'

'I am fool. I am such idiot.' Mr Kowalski smacked himself sharply on the side of the head. 'I knew this happen one day. You wait here. I get you drink.'

Mr Kowalski left, but was back a moment later with a glass of water. Alex sipped it gratefully.

'I'm sorry, Mr Kowalski,' he said. 'I know I shouldn't have –'

'No, no!' Mr Kowalski waved his hands. 'Is all my fault. You are young boy. You want to know why old man next door lives in house with curtains drawn and windows locked. You are curious. Of course you are.' He gave himself another smack on the head. 'I knew this happen one day.'

Alex was beginning to recover. 'What . . . what sort of snake, is it?' he asked.

'Is African python,' said Mr Kowalski. 'Biggest snake in the world.' There was a touch of pride in his voice as he spoke.

'Why . . . how . . . where did you get him?'

'Ah . . . Long time ago. Twenty years.' With a sigh Mr Kowalski sat himself on the carpet beside Alex, his back against the wall. 'When I come to this country, I have no family, no friends, no one. Only Saskia.'

'Saskia?'

Mr Kowalski nodded. 'Engineer on ship give him to me. I keep him in my pocket. Talk to him. Tell him all my worries. Ask what I should do. He sleep in bed with me. He curl up by my feet . . .' He smiled. 'He is good friend.'

'But then, time pass, and he grow bigger.' Mr

Kowalski's smile faded. 'He grow big, then more big, then more and more bigger. My daughter she say, "He is dangerous animal. Is against the law. Get rid of him!" But how can I? Saskia is friend. I cannot get rid of friend! My daughter she say, "I not visit you any more while you have snake. You choose." I say "OK, I choose snake."' Mr Kowalski let out a long breath. 'Then he eat dog.'

'A dog?' said Alex. 'He ate a dog?'

Mr Kowalski nodded. 'I try to keep him indoors. I close all windows and lock doors, but one day he escape to garden. Catch Mrs Penrose dog and eat it. So I put up fence and barbed wire. Try to keep animals away. And children. I not want him to eat children. So I feed him. Feed him lot of food so he is not hungry. But lot of food make him grow more big. I put up curtains at window, so no one see him. I make it dark so he move less, but . . . I don't know . . . is always *something* can go wrong.'

Mr Kowalski looked across at Alex. 'My sister she say give him to zoo, but how? If I call zoo, maybe they call police. Maybe I go to prison, I don't know. If I *know*, maybe I do it, but I think –'

Alex never heard what Mr Kowalski thought because at that moment the old man disappeared, along with his house and sitting room, and Alex was standing in front of the desk in his bedroom, with Callum beside him.

'I keep my eyes on Mr Kowalski,' Callum was saying. 'If I see him coming back to the house, I press Ctrl-Z.'

Alex took a moment to remember when he was.

'So why didn't you?'

'What?'

'Why didn't you press Ctrl-Z?' demanded Alex. 'Mr Kowalski came back to the house, but you didn't do anything!'

Callum thought for a moment. 'Is this one of those "you've already done it and come back again" moments?' he asked.

'Yes,' said Alex, 'only I nearly didn't come back at all. What happened?'

'I don't know,' said Callum. 'I haven't done anything yet, remember?' He frowned. 'But I *must* have pressed Ctrl-Z, mustn't I? Otherwise you wouldn't have come back from wherever you've been.'

Alex realized this had to be true. 'All right, maybe you *did* press it, but not until it was nearly too late,' said Alex.

'Well, I'm sorry,' said Callum, 'but if I didn't press it, it must have been because I was struck by lightning or something. You know I wouldn't have left you there without a reason.'

'No, no, I know that . . .' Alex was beginning to recover. 'I'm sorry. I'm just a bit . . . You see, that snake nearly killed me.'

'A snake?' Callum's eyes widened. 'You were nearly killed by a snake?'

Alex took a deep breath and began telling Callum about the snake, about not being able to move, and about Mr Kowalski coming in from the garden, when his mother appeared at the door.

'I need someone to hold the exhaust in place while I screw in a bracket,' she said, looking at Alex. 'D'you mind?'

'Can I do it later?' asked Alex. 'Only I need to talk to Callum about –'

'Come on!' His mother briskly closed the lid of his computer with one hand and swept up Alex with the other. 'You can both come. It won't take long. Five minutes. Ten at the most.'

'I think I know why you didn't press the button now,' said Alex quietly as he and Callum followed his mother down to the garage.

Much later, as Alex was lying in bed that night going over the events of the day in his head before falling asleep, he wondered what he was going to do about Mr Kowalski. Twice now, at times of great danger, the old man had come to his rescue. He had saved Lilly from being burnt alive and now he had saved Alex from being crushed by a snake. Again, Alex faced the problem of how to thank him for doing something he didn't even know had happened.

It would be nice this time, Alex thought, to do something more than bake him a cake, and there was one thing he *could* do for his neighbour. The last thing Mr Kowalski had said, sitting on the floor of his living room, was that he wanted to know whether, if anyone found out about him having the snake, it meant he would go to prison.

And it couldn't be too difficult to get a piece of information like that . . .

Chapter Twelve

Alex rang the police straight after breakfast the following morning. He used the number you were supposed to use if it wasn't an emergency, gave his name and address, and asked what would happen to his neighbour if anyone found out that he was keeping an African python. Would the snake be confiscated and would the owner have to go to prison?

The answer was not good news. The woman on the phone told him that it was against the law to keep any exotic pet that was a danger to the public and that, yes, the penalties could involve confiscation, a fine and even imprisonment. Alex thanked her, put down the phone and went over to his computer.

The first thing he needed to do was go back

five minutes to before he had made the phone call, but when he turned on the laptop, nothing happened. He pressed the On switch several times, but the screen stayed completely blank and there was no little green light to say the power was on. Alex felt a brief moment of panic before he realized what had happened. In all the excitement last night, he had forgotten to turn the laptop off and now the battery had run down. All he had to do was plug it into the mains and then he could use Ctrl-Z.

Except that he couldn't find the lead. He searched his room for several minutes and then remembered he had left it at Callum's house the day before. Using Ctrl-Z took a lot of power and the laptop needed recharging at least every two or three days. It was no problem. He would walk round and get it.

'Wish your mother luck!' said his father, as Alex came downstairs.

Mrs Howard was standing by the front door, wearing a smart black suit, a white blouse and a slightly nervous expression.

'She's off to a job interview,' his father explained. 'But she's going to get this one, aren't you, love?' He beamed at his wife. 'Don't forget. If the car breaks down or anything, you ring and I'll come and pick you up.'

Alex waved his mother off from the pavement before walking up the road to Callum's house. To his surprise, there was no answer when he rang the front doorbell, nor when he walked round and knocked at the back. There was no car in the drive either and it was clear that the Bannisters had gone out. Alex waited a bit in case they had only gone down to the shops, but no one turned up.

He went next door to ask Mrs Penrose if she knew where they had gone, but she only knew that the Bannisters had all gone off in the car at about nine thirty. She had no idea when they might be back.

He hung around the house a bit longer before walking home to find a policeman waiting for him in the kitchen with Mr Howard.

'This is Constable Williams,' said his father. 'He says you rang the police half an hour ago.'

'Um . . . yes,' said Alex.

'You said on the phone . . .' Constable Williams consulted his notebook, '. . . that you wanted to know what would happen to your neighbour if he was found keeping a three-metre African python without a licence, and it had eaten a dog. Is that right?'

'Um . . . yes,' said Alex.

'Can I ask which neighbour you were worried about exactly?'

'It's not Mr Kowalski, is it?' Mr Howard was staring at his son. 'Is that who you meant?'

'Um . . . yes,' said Alex.

'You've seen this snake, have you?' asked the policeman.

'Um . . . yes,' said Alex.

He thought about lying, but there didn't seem to be any point. Once he got hold of the mains lead for his computer, none of this would have happened anyway, and in the meantime it would be useful to know for certain what the police would do about Mr Kowalski and his African python.

Constable Williams turned to Mr Howard. 'This Mr Kowalski lives at . . . ?'

'Number sixteen,' said Mr Howard. 'Next door.'

'Right.' The policeman put away his notebook. 'Well, I'll go and have a word with him. See what he says.' He smiled at Alex. 'Don't worry. You did the right thing!'

An hour later, there were three police cars in the road outside and a large van with bars on its windows. Alex watched from the sitting-room window as four burly policemen carried an enormous canvas bag the size of a tent containing Saskia the snake out of Mr Kowalski's house to the van. Mr Kowalski followed, looking rather pale, and Constable Williams put him in the back of one of the police cars. He looked very small and old and frail, and Alex couldn't help thinking that the sooner he could use Ctrl-Z to put everything back to how it had been the better.

He spent the rest of the morning cycling up and down the road outside Callum's house, waiting for his friend or any of the Bannister family to come home and let him into the house, but none of them did. When he finally went home for lunch, he found out why.

'Callum called while you were out,' said Mr Howard, when Alex came back to the kitchen. 'Bad news, I'm afraid. He says Lilly hurt her leg this morning, sliding down the stairs on a tea tray and they've taken her to hospital. They're worried it might start off the infection again. He said to tell you the accident happened at nine twenty-seven. He was very insistent I give you the exact time for some reason.'

'Oh,' said Alex. 'Thanks.'

'It's all happening this morning, isn't it?' said Mr Howard. 'Mr Kowalski gets arrested, Lilly winds up back in hospital . . . but at least we have one thing to celebrate.' He pointed to the table where he had set out a bottle of champagne and two glasses. 'Your mother got the job!'

'She did?'

'Yes. But she doesn't know that we know yet, so you'll have to pretend to look surprised when she tells us.' Mr Howard grinned happily. 'I used to work with the man in charge of the firm she's applying to, and he told me yesterday he was definitely giving her the job. Said he wasn't even bothering to interview anyone else, so this morning's just a formality!'

At least that was one part of the day he wouldn't have to change, Alex thought, but it turned out he was wrong. When his mother got home, she said that she had not been given the job after all.

'The man was very nice,' she said, standing in the hallway to change her shoes. 'He said he was sorry and I'd come very close, but there was a lot of competition. I suppose I just keep trying. I'm dying for a cup of tea. Can someone put the kettle on?'

'The man told you there was a lot of competition?' said Mr Howard.

'Yes . . . there were about a dozen of us being interviewed.' Mrs Howard pulled on a pair of slippers. 'Next time, eh?'

'You didn't even go, did you?' said Mr Howard in a low voice.

'What?'

'You didn't go to the interview at all, did you? You didn't turn up.'

'What are you talking about?' Mrs Howard gave an odd laugh. 'Of course I turned up. I told you . . .' She stopped and let out a long, deep breath. 'No,' she said slowly. 'No, I didn't go to the interview.'

Alex waited for his father to explode, but his voice was very quiet when he spoke. 'Can I ask why?'

'Because I didn't want the job, all right?' Mrs Howard spoke sharply. 'It's my life, isn't it? It's my decision. I think I should at least be allowed to decide for myself what job I want!'

She walked through to the kitchen and turned on the kettle. Mr Howard stared after her and Alex thought he was going to start shouting, but he didn't. Instead he walked into the dining room and closed the door. Mrs Howard came out of the kitchen and went upstairs, leaving Alex alone in the hallway. It was very quiet, but it wasn't a good quiet. Alex would almost have preferred it if they'd been shouting.

As he went upstairs to his room, he couldn't help feeling that the sooner he got the lead for his computer and pressed Ctrl-Z the better.

When he could use his laptop again, Alex knew he would be able to put everything right. He could go back to before he had phoned the police so that Mr Kowalski wasn't arrested. He could go back to before Lilly hurt her leg and warn Callum not to let her slide down the stairs on a tray. And he could go back to before his mother left for her interview and tell her that Dad knew she was going to get the job. That way at least she wouldn't pretend she'd been to the interview when she hadn't.

All it needed was for Callum to come back from the hospital . . . but he didn't. Alex called round to the Bannisters' house every half-hour or so through the afternoon to see if there was any sign of him, but there never was.

At five o'clock, Mrs Penrose, Callum's neighbour, came back from a walk with both Jennings and Mojo. She said Mr Bannister had rung from the hospital to say there had been complications and they were staying until things were sorted out. He had asked her to look after Mojo until they got back, but had no idea of when that might be. That was when Alex thought he should try to get a mains connector cable from somewhere else.

At home, his parents were still not speaking to each other, and they weren't talking to Alex much either. His mother was in the garage, polishing the chrome on her Triumph, and didn't seem to hear when he asked if she knew where he could get hold of a new cable. He had to repeat the question twice before she answered that she had no idea. His father, sitting in his office staring blankly out of the window was no help either. He said it was too late to go to the shops and no, they didn't have a spare cable that fitted the socket on the laptop.

The situation was serious, but not desperate, Alex thought. One of the things he had learnt in the weeks since he had discovered Ctrl-Z was not to worry unnecessarily. What was there to worry about when you had a machine that could go back to before anything bad happened and make sure it didn't? As long as Callum came back before midnight, all the day's disasters could still be undone.

And even if he didn't, there was always Plan B.

Plan B had been at the back of Alex's mind from the start. He still thought the most likely thing would be for the Bannisters to get back from the hospital so that he could retrieve the cable, but if they didn't, all he would have to do was break into their house and take it. He had thought of doing it that afternoon, but decided in the end to wait. If he was going to do anything illegal while the laptop was temporarily out of action, it would be better to wait until dark.

It was ten o'clock at night when Alex got up, crept downstairs to the kitchen, took a torch from the drawer, pulled a coat on over his pyjamas and quietly let himself out of the back door.

Callum's house was in darkness when he got there, and there was no car in the drive. The Bannisters were still at the hospital. Alex made his way round to the back of the house. Standing on the patio, trying to decide which window to break to get in, he realized there was no need. In their haste to leave that morning, Mr Bannister had left the patio door slightly ajar. All Alex had to do was push it open and step inside.

By the light of the torch, he climbed the stairs to Callum's bedroom. That was where he had left the lead plugged into the wall and, with luck, it would still be there.

It wasn't.

Callum must have moved it. Alex began searching the room, looking for anywhere his friend might have put it. Ten minutes later, he was still looking, the torch battery was giving out and Alex drew the curtains and turned on the light, hoping that no one outside would notice.

In the next half-hour, he turned Callum's room upside down. He searched every drawer and cupboard, looked in and under the bed, went through all the boxes stored in the wardrobe and even pulled the bookcase away from the wall in case the wire had fallen behind it. But it hadn't. There was no sign of the lead anywhere.

He was beginning to worry. He should have

come here earlier, he thought, whatever the risk. He should have tried to phone Callum at the hospital. He should have got his father to take him into town straight after lunch to buy another lead, and he definitely should have remembered to turn off his computer the night before . . . There were so many things he should have done.

In a mood of increasing desperation, he began looking in other parts of the house. He went downstairs and searched the living room and the hallway. He turned on all the lights and looked in the kitchen and the dining room and then went back and searched all the rooms all over again. He was still frenziedly searching when he heard the grandfather clock in the Bannisters' hallway striking twelve.

He turned on the television in the sitting room to double-check the time, but there was no mistake. Midnight had passed. As he had learnt the first day he had got the computer, you could change the time with Ctrl-Z, but not the date. You could only use it to wind back events within the space of the same day. He sat down in an armchair, feeling suddenly very tired. There was no point looking for the lead any more. Even if he found it, it was too late.

Mr Kowalski's arrest, Lilly's leg, his parents not

talking . . . There was nothing he could do about any of them now.

The day was over and there was no going back.

Alex let himself in through the back door, hung up his coat, and was tiptoeing through the hall when the door to the sitting room opened.

'Alex?' Mr Howard stood in the doorway in his dressing gown. Behind him, Alex could see pillows and a blanket laid out on the sofa.

'You couldn't sleep either, eh?' His father put a hand on Alex's shoulder. 'Come on. Let's cheer ourselves up with a hot drink.'

In the kitchen, while his father busied himself collecting two mugs and heating up milk in the microwave, Alex couldn't help thinking that it was going to take more than a cup of hot chocolate to cheer him up at this point. It was probably the worst day of his life. Worse than the time he had got lost on the beach when he was three years old, and even worse than the time . . .

He stopped. In front of him, lying openly on the kitchen worktop, was the black wire of the power lead for his computer.

He picked it up. 'How . . . how did this get here?'

'Mrs Penrose brought it round.' His father was watching the milk through the door of the microwave. 'It's the power lead for your computer. You left it at Callum's.'

'When did she bring it round?'

'About nine thirty, I think.' Mr Howard was spooning the chocolate powder into the mugs. 'Callum rang her from the hospital. He was worried you might need it, so he asked her to pick it up from his house and bring it over. They're all staying at the hospital overnight to keep an eye on Lilly.'

'Why . . .' Alex was still staring at the wire. 'Why didn't you tell me?'

'You'd gone to bed by then, hadn't you!' Mr Howard carried the mugs over to the table. 'And it seemed to me like you needed your sleep. Especially after a day like today.' He sat down with a sigh. 'Because it's not been the best day for any of us, really, has it?' He sipped his drink. 'Not the best day at all.'

Alex stared miserably at the lead in his hands. He hadn't thought it was possible to feel worse than he had when he'd heard midnight strike on the clock in Callum's house, but he'd been wrong. He'd been wrong about so many things all through the day. He'd made so many silly mistakes.

And the computer lead had been sitting in the kitchen for the last three hours. If he had known. If only he had known . . .

'It's all my fault,' he said miserably.

'What is?'

'Everything,' said Alex. 'Lilly's accident, Mr Kowalski, you and Mum . . . it's all my fault.'

'Well, I think you might be exaggerating slightly there.' Mr Howard put down his mug and looked across at his son. 'Mr Kowalski was arrested for keeping a dangerous animal – his fault, not yours. Lilly falling downstairs certainly didn't have anything to do with you. And as for your mother and me . . . I'm afraid we managed to mess up that one all on our own.' He gave Alex a tired smile. 'From where I'm sitting, you look like the only one today that's got nothing to blame himself for at all.'

Unfortunately, Alex knew it wasn't true. If he'd just been a bit more careful, none of the day's disasters would have happened. If he'd checked the computer was working before he'd rung the police . . . If he hadn't left the lead round at Callum's . . . If he'd tried earlier to get a replacement . . .

He had made so many mistakes.

CHAPTER THIRTEEN

At breakfast the next morning, Alex's parents were still not talking – not to each other at any rate. They said the odd word to Alex, but otherwise they both behaved as if the other person didn't exist. It was not a pleasant atmosphere, and it was a relief when his mother went off to work, his father announced that he was going out for a walk and Alex found himself alone in the house.

He badly wanted to talk to someone about what had happened, but there wasn't anyone to talk to. The only person who might have understood was Callum, but Alex felt so guilty about Lilly that, even if his friend was back from the hospital, he couldn't face seeing him. And there wasn't anyone else who knew about Ctrl-Z and who might under-stand how he felt and . . .

And then it occurred to him that there *was* one other person who knew about Ctrl-Z. Godfather John. If he sent him an email, Alex thought, and told him what had happened, he might be able to give some advice, and he was on his way upstairs to turn on his laptop when there was a knock at the front door.

Standing on the step was a big man dressed almost entirely in black. He wore a long black coat over a black shirt and trousers, with polished black shoes on his feet and a wide black hat on the grizzled grey hair on his head. Above the thick grey beard and the heavily lined face, a pair of twinkling black eyes looked down at Alex.

'Hello, Alex,' said the man, his voice booming down the hall.

It took Alex a moment to realize who it was. He couldn't remember meeting the man before, but he recognized the face. There was a photograph of it on the mantelpiece in the front room.

'Godfather John?'

'That's me!' The man came striding into the hallway. 'I got your email and it sounded like you could do with some help!'

'Email?' Alex frowned. 'I haven't written one yet.'

'Yes, I know. You send it in about an hour.' Godfather John had taken a small palmtop computer from his pocket and studied it. 'But as I was going to call in anyway, I used Ctrl-Z to get here early.'

Alex looked at the tiny computer. 'Is that . . .'

'It's the new model,' said Godfather John. 'Easier to carry around. That's why I passed the old one on to you. Thought you might have a chance to make some useful mistakes!' He beamed down at Alex. 'So where are your parents?'

Alex explained that his mother was at work and that his father had gone out for a walk.

'Excellent!' said Godfather John. 'That'll give us a chance to talk!'

In the kitchen, while Godfather John made himself some coffee and a plate of sandwiches, Alex started to tell him what had happened the previous day, but his godfather insisted that he start the story right from the beginning. He wanted to know everything that had happened, he said, everything that Alex had done, from the first time he had used the laptop. And he listened attentively and sympathetically, only occasionally interrupting with a question or a comment, as Alex described his adventures with Ctrl-Z.

Some of the stories made him smile, one or two made him laugh, but he was particularly pleased, for some reason, when Alex told him what had happened when he sprayed Sophie Reynolds with foam from a fire extinguisher. He made Alex go over the whole story twice, and when he'd finished, banged his fist enthusiastically on the table.

'Now that is *exactly* the sort of mistake I was hoping you'd make,' he said, his smile broader than ever. 'Well done!'

The smile faded slightly when Alex finally got to describe the events of the previous day – with Mr Kowalski getting arrested, Lilly breaking her leg and his parents having their row about his mother not going to the job interview.

'The thing is,' said Alex, 'I could have stopped all of it happening. I *should* have stopped it. And I feel awful.'

'Yes . . .' Godfather John nodded sympathetically. 'It's not easy, is it?'

'Is there anything you could do to help?' asked Alex.

'How do you mean?'

'Well . . . I was wondering if you could go back to yesterday and change things.' Alex pointed to the palmtop on the table. 'Can the new machine do something like that?'

'Sorry,' said his godfather. 'No, it can't.'

'Isn't there *anything* I can do?'

'Well, there's only one thing you ever have to do when you've made a mistake,' said Godfather John, 'and that's decide not to do it again.'

'Oh,' said Alex, disappointed.

'And apologize to anyone who got hurt, of course.' Godfather John put the last bit of sandwich in his mouth and washed it down with his third mug of coffee before leaning back in his chair. 'I'm not sure why that bit's important, but it seems to be part of the process.' He pointed his finger at Alex. 'So my advice is to get round to Mr Kowalski, say you're sorry and promise not to report him to the police again. Not without a working Ctrl-Z, anyway.'

The last thing Alex wanted to do was go anywhere near number 16. He wasn't sure if Mr Kowalski knew that he was the one who had called the police or not, but if he *did* know, he would almost certainly be very angry. A picture of the old man shooting at the dog in his garden as he shouted at it to go away flashed into Alex's head . . .

'What happens,' he said, 'if I go round, and Mr Kowalski's really cross?'

Godfather John gave a chuckle. 'Oh, I think you'll be all right!'

'You think?'

'In fact I'm sure of it,' said Godfather John confidently. 'I've got this, remember?' He held up his palmtop. 'I wouldn't be advising you to do something that I didn't know was going to turn out OK, would I?'

Alex thought about this for a moment. 'Right. And then you think I should do the same thing with Callum . . . and my parents?'

'I definitely think you should have a word with Callum – he's your friend, after all.' Godfather John paused for a moment before continuing. 'But I don't think you should say anything to your parents. Because you don't really have anything to apologize to them for, do you? As your father said, they seem to have messed that one up all on their own.' He gave another throaty chuckle. 'It sounds to me like they've been making much bigger mistakes than you have!'

Alex was slightly confused. 'You keep making it sound like making a mistake is a good thing,' he said.

'But of course it is!' Godfather John beamed at him across the table. 'That's why I sent you the laptop, remember? So you could make lots of mistakes.'

'Yes,' said Alex. 'I know that's what you said. I just never understood why . . .'

'I said it because we *have* to make mistakes, Alex. All of us. It's how we learn!' Godfather John's eyes glinted under his bushy eyebrows as he spoke.

'Think of when you were a baby learning to walk. You took your first step, you fell over, you got up, took another step, you fell over again ... And that's how any of us learns anything. By trying it, getting it wrong and trying it again.'

He leant across the table towards Alex. 'What would have happened if you'd decided after the first mistake to give up learning to walk because you were getting it wrong? You'd have been stuck sitting down for the rest of your life, wouldn't you! No, no ...' Godfather John shook his head firmly. 'Nothing to be ashamed of in making a mistake. The mistakes are how we learn and grow – and the learning and the growing are what we're all here to do in the first place, aren't they!'

Alex opened his mouth to answer, but Godfather John was already pulling him to his feet. 'You'd better get round and see Mr Kowalski,' he said, looking at his watch. 'Your father's going to be home in two and a half minutes and he and I need to have a little talk.'

Mr Kowalski gave Alex a friendly wave when he saw him coming up the path. He was standing on a stepladder by the open window using a hammer to pull out the nails that had once held the curtains closed so that nobody could see inside.

'Door is open, Alex!' he called. 'Come on in!'

Alex walked through to the sitting room, which looked very different now that the curtains at either end of the room had been taken down. The windows were wide open and a fresh breeze was blowing through from the garden.

'Is good to see you!' Mr Kowalski climbed down from the ladder and gestured Alex to a chair. 'You hear what happen yesterday?'

'Yes, I did. And that's why –'

'Bad business!' Mr Kowalski shook his head. 'Very bad. But we not talk about it. Instead, we eat cake!' Mr Kowalski crossed to the table and picked up a tin. 'Is Polish cake. Called *szarlotka*. I make it specially for you!'

'Mr Kowalski,' said Alex, 'I've come to say sorry.'

'Sorry?' Mr Kowalski was busily cutting a large slice of cake and putting it on a plate. 'Why you sorry?'

Alex wished that Mr Kowalski would stop being so nice. He almost wished he would go back to being grumpy and bad-tempered instead of looking at him, as he did now, with such kindly concern on his face.

'I came to say sorry –' Alex took a deep breath. – 'because it was me that told the police about the snake.'

For several long seconds Mr Kowalski said

nothing. He stared down at Alex with a frown of puzzled incomprehension.

'You? You tell police?'

'Yes.' Alex could not remember when he had ever felt so uncomfortable. 'I'm sorry. I didn't mean to get you into trouble. I just wanted to find out what would happen. I never meant for them to arrest you and take away the snake . . .'

'How you know about Saskia?' demanded Mr Kowalski.

'Well, I-I saw him.'

'When?'

'I-I came into your house one day . . .' Alex could feel himself blushing. 'When you were out.'

'Ah . . .' The old man let out a long sigh and sat slowly on a chair.

'I'm really sorry, Mr Kowalski. I didn't mean to do anything that hurt you.'

Mr Kowalski did not answer, but stared at the carpet for some time without speaking. Finally, he made a little gesture with his hands. 'Is not so bad,' he said.

'Really?'

'Police tell me no charges. No fine. No prison.'

'Oh,' said Alex. 'What about . . .'

'Saskia gone to zoo. They very pleased to have him. I think he be happy there. And they tell me I visit whenever I like.'

147

'Oh. Good.'

'I ring my daughter this morning and tell her. She coming to stay. With my granddaughter.' He gestured to the room behind him. 'Lot of cleaning to do.'

'Yes, I suppose there is,' said Alex. 'Can I help?'

In the circumstances, it seemed the least he could do and for the next hour he helped Mr Kowalski as he hoovered and dusted and carried the old newspapers that had once been the bedding for an African python down to a bonfire at the end of the garden.

Halfway through, when they were having a drink and some of the Polish cake – which was delicious – Mr Kowalski said, 'Alex? When my granddaughter come, you will visit and say hello, yes?'

'Sure,' said Alex. 'And I wanted to ask, when you go and see Saskia at the zoo, would you take me with you?'

The old man's face creased into a smile.

'Is a promise, my young friend,' he said. 'Is a promise.'

When Alex rang the doorbell at number 27, it was answered by Callum's father. Alex asked him how Lilly was.

'Not so bad, thank you,' said Mr Bannister. 'They think she's going to be all right. I'm going in later with Callum, but I thought I'd clear up a bit first. You heard about the burglary?'

'Burglary!' said Alex. 'No. What happened?'

'Someone broke in while we were out last night,' said Mr Bannister. 'When we got back this morning, the house was a real mess. Nothing missing, fortunately. The police think it was local kids messing around. They got in through the patio door.' He glanced down at Alex. 'You want to see Callum?'

'If that's all right,' said Alex.

'I'd be glad if you would. He could do with a visitor to cheer him up.' Mr Bannister headed back to the kitchen. 'He was very upset about yesterday. Almost as if he thought the accident was his fault!'

'It *was* my fault,' said Callum, when Alex went upstairs and explained what had happened the day before. He lay on his bed, gazing gloomily up at the ceiling. 'If only I'd remembered that I had the cable! Or rung you earlier. Or told Mrs Penrose to make sure she gave it to you personally . . . I can't believe I was so stupid!'

'I've been talking to your dad,' said Alex. 'He says you were the one who found Lilly. He says if you hadn't raised the alarm when you did, it could have been much worse.'

Callum gave a shrug. 'I still shouldn't have made the mistake about the power lead.'

'My godfather says we all make mistakes,' said Alex. 'He says we're supposed to. He says it's how we learn.'

'Really?' said Callum. He thought for a moment. 'Is that supposed to help? Because it doesn't.'

And Alex had to agree that it didn't much.

'How did it go?' asked Godfather John, when Alex got back to the house.

'Not as bad as I expected,' said Alex.

'Good, good.' Godfather John was in the hall, pulling his coat on, and Alex could see his father busy in the kitchen putting plates and cups in the sink.

'I'm driving your dad into town now,' said Godfather John. 'We're going to see your mother. Do you want to come with us?'

'Well . . .' said Alex.

'Of course you do!' Godfather John clapped a hand on his shoulder and then added in a lower voice, 'You don't have to worry!' He gestured to the palmtop in his pocket. 'I've done this bit already and it goes *terribly* well!'

CHAPTER FOURTEEN

The garage where Mrs Howard worked looked different from the last time Alex had seen it, soon after his mother started there. Then, the reception area had been dirty and dimly lit. Now it was clean, freshly painted, there were comfortable chairs for customers to sit on as they waited, a machine that provided free coffee, and relaxing music played quietly in the background.

Looking around, however, there was no sign of Mrs Howard.

'If you're looking for Lois,' said a middle-aged woman standing by the reception desk, 'she's in the workshop.' She pointed to a glass window behind the desk through which they could see several men in overalls working on a variety of cars. One of them had been raised up on a ramp, and Mrs Howard was standing underneath it with one of the mechanics.

'She won't be long,' said the woman. 'She's just sorting out my brake fluid.'

Alex watched as his mother peered at the underneath of the car, tapped at a section of the metal with a screwdriver and tugged at a section of pipe further along. She moved with the easy confidence of someone who knew exactly what she was doing, and when she spoke to the mechanic, Alex noticed, he listened attentively to what she was saying.

'I've not been here before.' Godfather John was addressing the middle-aged woman at the reception desk. 'Can I ask . . . is this a reliable garage?'

'It's first class,' said the woman, 'but if you want anything special done, make sure you speak to Lois. She's the one in charge.'

'In charge?' Alex's father had stepped forward. 'I thought she was the receptionist?'

'Oh, she's everything, really,' said the woman, 'since Mr Fothergill had his heart trouble. Receptionist, chief mechanic, general manager . . .'

Mr Howard frowned. 'Mr Fothergill's been ill?

'He's been out of it for almost six months now,' said the woman. 'That's why Lois took over. This is all her!' The woman gestured round the reception area. 'You should have seen this place before! But if you want to speak to her, you need to get here before three thirty. She has to go home early most days, to look after her son.'

'So you'd recommend this place, would you?' asked Godfather John.

'I wouldn't go anywhere else,' said the woman firmly. Her face clouded for a moment. 'Though of course I may have to.'

'Really? Why's that?'

'Word is that Lois is leaving.' The woman let out a long sigh. 'She's going to be an accountant. There's a lot of us will miss her, I can tell you, but I suppose we just have to make the most of her while she's here!'

Godfather John thanked her for her advice and led both Alex and his father outside. Standing on the garage forecourt, he turned to Mr Howard.

'Well?' he said.

Mr Howard looked rather dazed. 'You're right,' he said eventually. 'I . . . I had no idea.'

Godfather John patted him on the shoulder. 'Of course you didn't. So you'll do it?'

'Well . . .' Mr Howard looked nervously back into the garage where his wife had come out of the workshop and was talking to the woman waiting at the desk. 'I suppose. If it's what she wants.' He looked at Godfather John. 'You're quite sure it *is* what she wants?'

'Quite sure,' said Godfather John. 'But don't take my word for it. Go and ask her!'

'Yes.' Mr Howard took a deep breath and braced his shoulders. 'Yes, I'll do that.' And he walked back into the garage.

'Take as long as you like,' Godfather John called after him. 'I'll look after Alex!'

Alex was not quite sure what was happening, but he had a feeling that whatever it was, it was important. He wanted to follow his father back into the garage, but Godfather John steered him firmly back towards the car.

'Best thing you and I can do is keep out of the way,' he said. 'With a bit of luck, he'll get it right this time!'

'Get what right?' asked Alex. 'I don't understand. What's he supposed to be saying to Mum?'

'Well,' Godfather John pulled open the car door and sat himself down inside. 'I suppose you have a right to know.' He waited until Alex had climbed in the other side. 'Your father's been trying to help your mother get a job as an accountant, and he's only just realized that's not what she wants to do.'

'Isn't it?' said Alex. His mother had been planning and preparing for a career in accountancy for as long as he could remember. 'Are you sure? She's been saying that's what she wants for years.

She and Dad are going to set up a partnership together.'

'That's what she *did* want, originally,' Godfather John agreed, 'but in the last year she's changed her mind. She's found something else she'd rather do instead.'

'Oh,' said Alex, and inside his head, all sorts of pieces suddenly slotted together like bits of a jigsaw. The way his mother had looked while she was checking over the underside of the car on the ramp. All the things the woman at the desk had said about how his mother was really running the garage. How she had spent the last two years doing up a Triumph TR4. And how everyone in the close came to her when something went wrong with their cars.

'She wants to work in a garage,' he said, and he couldn't understand why he hadn't realized this before.

'That's the way it looks to me.' Godfather John adjusted the rear-view mirror so that he could see what was going on behind him in the reception area.

'If she wants to work in a garage,' said Alex, 'why didn't she say so?'

'Well, that was her big mistake, of course.' Godfather John was still watching the mirror. 'Not telling your father. But to be fair, she probably didn't know herself at first, and then, when she did, she was worried it might upset him. I mean, as you said, they've been planning the accountancy thing for years. Invested a lot of time and money. It can't have been easy after all that to come out and say she'd changed her mind.'

Alex thought of all the hours Dad had spent helping Mum through one exam after another, all so that one day they could set up in business together. The idea of telling him, when the work was almost done, that she wanted to do something else must have been even harder than telling Mr Kowalski that you were the one who had called the police.

'And your dad's mistake was to keep pushing her into something she didn't want,' said Godfather John. 'That's what all the arguments were really about, of course. All the rows about screwdrivers and tea towels. What was really happening was that your father thought your mother should be pushing forward, and your mother didn't want to.' He still hadn't taken his eyes off the mirror. 'So now he's telling her that if she wants to work in a garage, that's fine with him and he doesn't mind at all. Well, not too much.'

'Will that make everything OK?' asked Alex.

'It should do, if he gets it right.' His godfather smiled at Alex. 'And if he doesn't, I'll take him back and make him do it again.'

Alex turned in his seat. Through the rear window he could see his parents sitting together on two of the reception chairs, deep in conversation. It wasn't easy to tell how things were going. They were talking very animatedly, but they weren't arguing or shouting, which had to be good. Then Mum seemed to be crying, which was a bit alarming, but no, a moment later she was laughing as well as crying and then she reached out to Dad and hugged him, held him really tightly as if she was determined never to let him go, and they were both laughing now ...

'Oh yes!' Godfather John smiled. 'That looks very promising!' He turned to Alex. 'Come on, time to get you home.'

By the time they got back to the house in Oakwood Close, it was nearly one o'clock.

'Lunchtime,' said Godfather John, 'and you're having it with Mr Kowalski.'

'Am I?' said Alex.

'Callum's going to come over in a minute and tell you.' Godfather John turned off the engine. 'He's very excited because Lilly's coming home from hospital this afternoon. He tells you that, and then he tells you you're invited to lunch. If I go into the house with you, I get invited too, but if you don't mind I won't do it again.' He yawned. 'I have to be in Rome by five o'clock.'

'Again?' said Alex. 'You mean you've done the lunch already?'

'Twice,' said Godfather John. He held up his palmtop. 'And the food is wonderful. Though you might want to steer clear of the *galabki*. Lot of cabbage involved in that one.'

'Oh,' said Alex. 'Right.'

'And after lunch you and Callum and Mishka – that's Mr Kowalski's granddaughter, you like her a lot – have a really great afternoon. Apart from when Callum smashes his hand on a brick, but you can sort that one out, can't you? With the laptop?'

It was odd, Alex thought, to be with someone who had already done most of your day and knew what was going to happen. It made him realize how strange the past few weeks must have been for Callum, but it was also reassuring to be told that everything was going to turn out all right.

'Your parents get back about half three, but don't expect to see too much of them until this evening.' Godfather John was still talking. 'Your father will be going over the account books from the garage, working out some sort of deal so your mother can take over properly. You'll find they're both very excited about it. And so they should be, of course!'

'Are they really going to be all right now?' asked

Alex. 'Mum and Dad, I mean? Are they going to be happy?'

'Very happy, I'd say!' Godfather John nodded vigorously. 'People usually are when they're doing what they want to do.'

'And there won't be any more arguments?'

'Definitely no more arguments!' said Godfather John. 'Until they make their next mistake . . .'

'Oh . . .' Alex felt a twinge of disappointment. 'You think they'll make another one?'

'Bound to, I'm afraid,' said his godfather sympathetically. 'We all do, remember? All of us. All the time.'

'Even you?'

'Oh yes. Every day.' Godfather John leant back in his seat. 'But like I said, it's not something to get too upset about. Because making mistakes is what we're supposed to do.' He put a hand on Alex's shoulder. 'Your parents will make more mistakes, so will you, so will I, but we don't need to worry because –'

'Because making mistakes is how we learn,' Alex finished for him.

'Exactly!' Godfather John smiled, and then reached down to press the button beside him that opened the car windows.

'Guess what!' Callum was standing on the pavement, bending down to speak to Alex. 'Go on, guess! You'll never guess!' He looked and sounded much more cheerful than when Alex had seen him that morning.

'You've heard that Lilly's coming home this afternoon and Mr Kowalski has invited us to lunch,' said Alex.

'How . . . how did you know that?' Callum frowned. 'Have you done today already?'

'I haven't,' said Alex, 'but my godfather has.'

'Oh!' Callum grinned happily at Godfather John. 'Hi!' He turned back to Alex. 'Mr Kowalski's got his granddaughter here and you know she can break bricks with one hand? She's this amazing karate expert. You have to come and see!'

'I will in a second,' said Alex. 'I just have to say goodbye.'

'Well, I think I've told you everything,' said Godfather John, as Callum walked back to the house. 'Your parents get back at three thirty, don't eat the *galabki*, look after your friend when he tries to do the brick thing . . .' He turned to Alex. 'Anything else we need to go over?'

'I don't think so,' said Alex, 'except . . . thank you. For everything. Sorting out Mum and Dad. Me and Mr Kowalski. Telling me what to do. Everything, really. It was amazing!'

'Oh, it was nothing!' said Godfather John, but he looked rather pleased.

'And thank you for the laptop as well,' Alex went on. 'It was a brilliant present. Really. The best ever.'

'Aha! You wait till you see what I've got for your next birthday!' Godfather John gave a little chuckle. 'You're not frightened of heights, I hope, because that'll be another one to keep quiet from your parents!' He turned the key in the ignition. 'Now, if there's nothing else, I really will –'

'There was one thing,' said Alex.

'Yes?'

'You remember you said, when I tried to win the lottery, that it wouldn't work, but there were twenty-seven other ways I could use Ctrl-Z to make a lot of money if I wanted?'

'Yes?'

'Well, I wondered if you could tell me what some of them are?'

Godfather John considered this, then reached into his jacket pocket for a paper and pen.

'I'll give you the first three,' he said. 'But you'll have to work out the others on your own.'

Standing on the pavement, Alex read what his godfather had written. The first idea was so simple, he was amazed he hadn't thought of it himself, and the second one was . . . was clever. He'd need someone like Callum to help him do it, but even so it shouldn't be too difficult.

A toot of the horn made him look up. Godfather John was moving away, waving with one hand out of the window as he left. And as he disappeared off down the road, Alex could hear him saying something. The words were almost drowned in the noise of the engine, but Alex could just make them out.

'Have fun,' his godfather was calling. 'And make lots of mistakes!'

And that is exactly what Alex has been doing ever since.

AN ANCIENT TOMB . . .
A TERRIBLE CURSE . . .
COULD NICHOLAS BE

THE
UNLUCKIEST
BOY IN
THE
WORLd ?

ANDREW NORRISS

puffin.co.uk

ANDREW NORRISS

tHe
toUCHStoNe

The Touchstone has all the answers.
The trick is Knowing the right question.

puffin.co.uk

ANDREW NORRISS

AQUILA

Where does IT come from?

What does IT do?

IT's a spaceship from the past –
but can IT change the future?

Winner of the Whitbread Children's Book Award
and Silver Smarties Prize

puffin.co.uk